ABOUT THIS BOOK

MISS HICKORY
Carolyn Sherwin Bailey

Most dolls lead a comfortable but unadventurous life. This was true of Miss Hickory until the early fall day that her owner, Ann, moved from her New Hampshire home to attend school in Boston—leaving Miss Hickory behind. For a country woman whose body is an apple-wood twig and whose head is a hickory nut, the prospect of spending a New Hampshire winter alone is frightening indeed. This fascinating story tells how, with the help of some unusual neighbors, she survived those trying months.

MISS HICKORY

BY CAROLYN SHERWIN BAILEY

With Lithographs by Ruth Gannett

PUFFIN BOOKS

PUFFIN BOOKS

A Division of Penguin Books USA Inc.
375 Hudson Street, New York, New York 10014
Penguin Books Ltd, 27 Wrights Lane, London W8 5TZ (Publishing & Editorial) and
Harmondsworth, Middlesex, England (Distribution & Warehouse)
Penguin Books Australia Ltd, Ringwood, Victoria, Australia
Penguin Books Canada Ltd, 10 Alcorn Avenue, Toronto, Ontario, Canada M4V 3B2
Penguin Books (N.Z.) Ltd, 182–190 Wairau Road, Auckland 10, New Zealand

First published by The Viking Press 1946
Viking Seafarer Edition published 1968
Reprinted 1971, 1972
Published in Puffin Books 1977
18   20   19

Library of Congress Cataloging in Publication Data

Bailey, Carolyn Sherwin, 1875-1961. Miss Hickory.
Summary: Relates the adventures of
a country doll made of an apple-wood
twig with a hickory nut for a head.
[1. Dolls—Fiction.   2. Country life—Fiction]
I. Gannett, Ruth Chrisman. II. Title.
PZ8.9.B16Mi8 [Fic] 77-1997
ISBN 0-14-030956-X

Printed in the United States of America
Set in Caledonia

CONTENTS

NOTE

Except for Ann and Timothy, who have been given those names in place of their own, all the characters in this book are real. They are all living, save Doe, in the places where they live in the book. They all still behave just as they do in the story.

THE CHARACTERS AS THEY APPEAR

MISS HICKORY: A country woman whose body was an apple-wood twig and whose head was a hickory nut.

CROW: Tough and wise. Also kindly.

GREAT-GRANNY BROWN: Who closed the Old Place and went to Boston for the winter.

MR. T. WILLARD-BROWN: A barn cat, and head-ratter.

COCK-PHEASANT: A famous berry-picker who deserted his wife.

CHIPMUNK: Spoiled and flighty.

SQUIRREL: Most forgetful.

HEN-PHEASANT: Sad and without pep.

COW: Who had a stomach-ache from overeating.

BARN-HEIFER: Cow's daughter who stayed at home.

WILD-HEIFER: Cow's daughter who roamed.

FAWN: Wild-Heifer's friend.

DOE: With God.

GROUND HOG: A surly man, and afraid of his shadow.

BULL FROG: Who lost his winter clothes.

ROBIN: A strutting fellow who felt important.

ANN: Who came home from school.

TIMOTHY: Of the farm next the Old Place.

1. CROW MAKES A CALL

Miss Hickory heard heavy footsteps, clump, clumping along the stones of the pasture, then approaching her lilac bush. Out of the corner of one sharp little black eye she could see a pair of large yellow feet but she did not turn her head. As a matter of fact Miss Hickory had difficulty in turning her head. It was a hickory nut that had grown with an especially sharp and pointed nose. Her eyes and mouth were inked on. Her body was an apple-wood twig formed like a body with two arms and two legs, hand and feet, as twigs sometimes grow. To this body Miss Hickory's nut head was glued. She wore a blue-and-white checked gingham dress. A white cap with ruffles was tied in a smart bow beneath her chin. Many persons, looking first at Miss Hickory, would have said that she was a country doll, made by Miss Keturah who kept the notions store in Hillsborough, and given to Ann. But not you or I. The tilt of her sharp little nose, her pursed mouth and her keen eyes were not those of a doll. You and I would have known Miss Hickory as the real person that she was.

A black shadow passed the doorsill of Miss Hickory's house. A coarse *caw* seemed intended to catch her attention, but she continued sweeping with her broom that was made of pine needles. She had just finished her tea and her acorn cup and saucer, neatly washed, stood on a shelf above the stove. A bed of discarded pullets' feathers covered with a bright quilt of patched sumac leaves was ready for pleasant dreams. Miss Hickory's house was made of corncobs, notched, neatly fitted together and glued. It stood beneath the lilac bush that was so sweet and purple when in bloom, so thickly green and cheerful with birds all summer long. If one had to live in town, Miss Hickory had always said, take a house under a lilac bush.

Soon, through her front door, the sunset would toss a few colored pieces from the orchard sky. Soon, too, the sun would drop like the biggest apple in the world, red and round, behind Temple Mountain that guarded the orchard spring, summer, autumn and winter, world without end. The sun set earlier now, for it was late September. Miss Hickory swept more briskly to warm herself. Thinking of cold weather made her shiver. But a large dark head with beady eyes and a long bill, thrust in through the window, stopped her.

Crow Makes a Call

"Are you at home, Miss Hickory?" Crow asked in his hoarse voice.

"Well, what do you think, if you ever do think?" she asked. "I heard your big yellow clodhoppers, and I saw you pass by. If you think there is one kernel of corn left in my house walls that you can peck out you are mistaken. You have eaten them all."

"Dear lady!" said Crow, stooping, entering and making himself at home. "Always so polite, so generous!"

A small smile seemed to move the wrinkles of Miss Hickory's face. "Here." She took from her pocket a few hard yellow kernels and held them out. Crow gobbled, choked, bowed low.

"Don't try to thank me," she urged. "You'll get the hiccoughs. What is the news? If there is any, you have heard it."

"Precisely why I am here, as they put it over the radio," he said. "News indeed, and it concerns you."

Miss Hickory sat down on her toadstool, spreading her skirts neatly to cover her ankles. Crow rested his wings comfortably, eased his toes and leaned against the wall. These two might spat and tiff, but they had fellow feelings. Crow made no pretensions; he was a country man. The earth owed him a living and so he helped himself to cherries and corn. Summer boarders, the bluebirds, thrushes, and larks, could fend for themselves, Crow felt, paying high prices for any berries and seeds that they got from his feeding ground. But he knew what was going on throughout the entire countryside. He was tough and weatherwise. He set the date for Old Crow Week in Hillsborough every spring, and so started the season with noisy promise. He could walk as well as fly, which meant that he got around more than most birds. He knew that Miss Hickory had once been part of a tree and he respected her for that ancestry. In certain ways they were alike. He waited for her to speak.

"Well?" she said at last.

Crow folded his wings over his stomach and pointed his beak at Miss Hickory.

"Great-granny Brown is closing this house for the winter. She plans to live in the Women's City Club on Beacon Hill, Boston, until spring." The house was full of stillness for a while, thick with thoughts that could not break it. His words stunned Miss Hickory. She could not speak.

"I know," Crow said at last, "that you expected to live another winter, house and all, on Great-granny Brown's kitchen windowsill. You expected Ann to drop in almost every day and bring you something useful, a little iron stove, a pot or a tin teakettle. But the entire family is going to Boston. Ann is to be put into school there." Crow rolled his eyes toward the ceiling, pretending to be shocked. Truly, however, he was enjoying himself. A love of gossip is hatched from every crow's egg.

Miss Hickory arose. She came close to him, her sharp little nose almost touching his face.

"They could not! They would not!"

"Ah, yes, Miss Hickory," he assured her. "Two-leggers who have been to Boston long for wings. Only we country people who can fly never feel the need of a city. Now, I once knew a starling who went to the Public Gardens in Boston for a visit, but—"

"Stop! Don't gabble." Miss Hickory twisted her hands in distress. "Come to the point."

"The point is yours, dear lady." Crow tapped her shoulder playfully with one wing-tip. "You have seen through Great-granny Brown's kitchen window how deep the snow-drifts are in New Hampshire. I'll wager that there were days when you could not see through the windows. The winters are long and hard here, Miss Hickory."

"What could one do?" she begged. She would not believe him yet.

"Don't feel too badly, as if they had forgotten you," he said kindly, "Ann has other matters than dolls to fill her mind now. Great-granny Brown was born and bred in New Hampshire. She expects you to be equal to any weather. You'll have to move, Miss Hickory."

"Where?" She went over to the window and looked west. There each year the forest, wild and deep, marched closer to the Old Place. They had both forgotten to admire the sunset. The afterglow, like a blanket of woven rainbows, had folded about Temple Mountain.

"Aye, that's the rub!" Crow replied hoarsely.

Miss Hickory stamped her foot. "Don't talk like a Poll-Parrot. Whatever you hear, either the radio or William Shakespeare, you repeat. You know you can't read a word."

Crow bowed his head humbly. "Right you are, but what

I meant was that we shall have to make a plan, and make it speedily. You can't live under a lilac bush all winter."

"We? This isn't your home. It belongs to me. I like it here. I can't move. Where would I take my stove, my pot and my teakettle, my cup and saucer and my bed? If I lived in a crows' nest, with no nice house furnishings and no good housekeeping . . ." She could not say any more. She could only look with love and fear at her four corncob walls.

"You give me an idea, Miss Hickory." Crow balanced himself on one foot and scratched his head with the other.

"I will have no idea of yours."

"But a little change is good for us all," Crow said smirkingly. "You must remember, dear lady, that you weren't born with a cup and saucer in your hand."

It was more than Miss Hickory could stand. She lost her temper. "I believe that this is all a piece of gossip on your part, Crow. I shall never believe that the Old Place is empty until I ask Mr. T. Willard-Brown. He will tell me the truth. As for you, Crow—" She stood as tall and brave as she could beside her door. "Get out of my house!" she ordered.

"As you wish." Crow walked in a dignified manner toward the door. "But don't worry. Something is bound to turn up!"

"I won't move!" she repeated as he stepped across the threshold. But he tapped her head lightly with his beak.

"Hardheaded, that's what you are!" And with that Crow walked off in the direction of the pine wood, he and the falling night one, in the color of dusk.

Miss Hickory put her twig hands up to her nut head.

Crow, she knew, was right. Her head was undoubtedly hard. She moved slowly about her house, lifting a stove lid to poke the red coals, turning down her bedspread. But as she comforted herself with these homely tasks, a feeling that she had never experienced before came to Miss Hickory. Perhaps it was caused by the sap that was still in her twig body. Perhaps it was the essence of the sweet nut inside the hard shell of her head. Whatever caused it, Miss Hickory began to cry. Tears came out of her eyes and rolled down her wrinkled cheeks. They fell so fast that she had to staunch them with her cap ties. It was dark then, so no one saw her break down. No one heard Miss Hickory sob, "It isn't true! I won't move! Mr. T. Willard-Brown will tell me tomorrow that I only had a bad dream."

2. MOON BEFORE SNOWFALL

"A GOOD day to finish my canning," Miss Hickory said to herself as she built up a wood fire and started toward the forest for berries.

It was a beautiful day, crisp but with warm sunshine that made her forget Crow's warning visit. Crow was so ready with raucous chit-chatter that she did not take him seriously. "He always has something to say and likes to hear himself say it," she reminded herself as she put a small rush basket over her arm and stepped briskly off on her twig feet. Although the torches that the goldenrod had lighted along the October road towered above Miss Hickory's head, she found her way easily in and out among them. Their brightness made her feel gay. Farther on the purple asters made a royal canopy beneath which she walked proudly until she came to the edge of the woods. She left the road and was at once in the deep green of the pines.

Miss Hickory's nose was as keen as a fox's. The smell of pine trees never failed to go to her head. She could not explain why, but when she was alone in the woods, sniffing rich earth, wandering through the lacy lanes of ferns, and smelling the pines, she felt like another person. She wished that she had time to dig up one of the tiny new hemlock trees to set out at the front of her corncob house, an idea that she had treasured for some time. But the cold of the woods, now that she had left the sunny road, made her realize that there would not be many more berrying days. She knelt down, dug away the leaves that already were making a thick covering on the earth.

It always surprised her to feel how warm the earth kept under the leaves, even on a cold day. She dug them aside, here and there, uncovering the vines that she wanted. It was as delightful to thrust her twig arms up to the elbows in the warm tangle as to sniff the woods. She began to pick the bright red berries and fill her basket. There was no time to lose, she knew. Cock-Pheasant lived close by and was a famous berry-picker.

Checkerberries first! They stood up straight, in plain sight on their stems, and could be picked fast. But for preserving and storing away in her acorn jugs for the winter, Miss

Hickory knew that checkerberry preserve needed a good
deal of sweetening, more honey than she had been able to
save that season. She picked a few checkerberry leaves.
They were tasty and crisp served with a cup of tea.

Next, the partridgeberries that ripened close to the
ground, little crimson balls in twins, two growing side by
side secretly on their low-lying running vine. Miss Hickory
canned partridgeberries whole in their own sweet juice. As
she finished gathering berries and started home with her
filled basket she remembered something that Cock-Pheasant
had once told her.

"When the partridgeberries are ripe," Cock-Pheasant had said, "it is only two full moons before the first snowfall."

When she came home, Miss Hickory saw that the entire front of her house was covered by the fat brindled haunches of Mr. T. Willard-Brown. He was enjoying the sunshine that trickled down through the bare lilac bushes and waving his long tail to and fro like a banner. He was a wandering barn cat, a hunter of renown, but Miss Hickory liked him. Mr. T. Willard-Brown lived a secret life closer to the ground than did Crow. He was a newsy man and willing to share his stories.

"You are late this morning," she told him.

"The milking was late," he explained. "I can't start the day without my regular breakfast of a dish of warm milk, right from the cow."

Miss Hickory set down her basket of berries, came close, and looked sharply into Mr. T. Willard-Brown's green eyes.

"That would have been a better story, my friend," she said, "if you had washed your face before you told it. There is a feather sticking out of your mouth." She flipped it off.

"Oh, my ears and whiskers," he exclaimed in mock chagrin. "However did I get into feathers so early in the morning? Now, if it had been teatime here at the Old Place and I had dropped in and someone had urged me to take a nap on one of those soft feather pillows—" He purred loudly to cover his embarrassment.

"Never mind," she said. "We all know your habits, Mr. T., and I am glad to see you this morning. Crow called a few days ago."

"Don't speak of him!" Mr. T. Willard-Brown spat. "I wouldn't eat crow on a wager. The last time I saw Crow he walked right toward me and said a bad word. I spat at him."

"If you ate crow occasionally you might be a better man," she told him. "What I was about to say when you interrupted me was that Crow spoke of the family as planning to leave Hillsborough for the winter. He said that Great-granny Brown was thinking of living at the Women's City Club on Beacon Hill, Boston, and Ann was going to school there. Nothing but hearsay on his part, of course."

Mr. T. Willard-Brown arose, stretched and yawned. "Not a plan, not hearsay, my love," he told Miss Hickory, "but the truth. They have gone!"

She listened without words, her eyes full of terror. He continued:

"You ought to get about more, Miss Hickory. All summer you have stayed here under the lilacs, only going to the woods for berries, or on Sunday when Jack-in-the-Pulpit preached. If you had gone around to the front of the house lately you would have seen trunks coming down from the attic."

"Gone!" she breathed at last. Now she knew that it was true. She would not let him see her cry. Instead she stamped her twig feet.

"It's all your fault, Mr. T. They had to leave to get away from *you,* scratching on doors and purring in the kitchen for milk. You are only a cat with a cat's ways. I shall tell all Hillsborough what your given name is, *Tippy,* because you have a white tip to your tail. Willard is for the barn where you were born. Brown is pretense. The hyphen is putting on airs. You are sly, Tippy. I always suspected it."

He purred loudly, curling his claws and smiling. "I am so famous a mouser that my given name and my humble birth are always overlooked. If you doubt Crow and me, why not go around to the front of the house and look in? See for yourself." He walked, with flowing tail, toward the barn.

Miss Hickory was unable to move for a space. She

watched Mr. T. Willard-Brown, swinging his sides and disappearing at last through the wide red doors of the barn. Then she walked slowly away from the lilac bush, the corncob house, her basket of berries. She skirted the garden, crossed the lawn and came to the pink rambler-rose trellis beside the front porch. Up the trellis she climbed, braving the sharp thorns, up, up, until she could peer underneath the crack of the window where the shade was not completely pulled down.

Blue Rocking Chair stood empty and still. The fireplace was boarded. The family Bible on the center-table was folded carefully in a white towel. The shining brass pendulum of the grandfather clock hung motionless and the hands pointed to eight o'clock. It must, by the shadow on the lawn sundial, be noon now. The Old Farmer's Almanac that had hung by a loop of string on the wall was gone. She had been alone, without knowing it, for some time.

She knew now that everything that Crow and Mr. T. Willard-Brown had told her was true. Her head would have whirled if it could. She felt too weak to hold on to the rose trellis, but she backed slowly down. Mr. T. Willard-Brown was waiting for her, having come softly around the corner of the house.

"Well, there you are, Miss Hickory," he purred. "Two of us in the same fix. Why not come over to the barn with me? It is to be kept open all winter and I have been offered a permanent position as head-ratter."

"I wasn't born to live in a barn," she told him desperately.

"Where then?" he asked.

"I am going home," she said. "Today I shall finish my canning."

"Home?" he smiled. "Amusing, that! I just passed your house and it was occupied. You know Chipmunk of course, who lives in the stone wall and has been so spoiled with gifts of peanuts that he expects to be supported? He has moved into your house, Miss Hickory. I should say that he is there for the winter. He was finishing his dinner when I saw him, your basket of berries."

3. UP McINTOSH LANE

M ISS HICKORY never remembered how long she sat on the ground under the rambler-rose trellis. If she had been living in her own home at the back of the house she might have cried, but that small corncob home, so cozy and familiar, was now occupied by Chipmunk. Here, with the open road in front, she was too proud to show her sorrow. More than sorrow, she felt despair. She became damp with the heavy dew and then stiff with the first frost. The wind whistling down from Temple Mountain whipped her wet skirts around her shivering legs. None of the few passers-by noticed her. Mr. T. Willard-Brown, warm and busy in the barn, gave her no thought. A light flurry of snow powdered her cap.

But one day, when Miss Hickory was sure that her end was near, down the road from the orchard, walking briskly, came Crow. Would he, too, pass her by? No. Crow turned into the front path and approached. He came close to the spot where Miss Hickory huddled under the poor shelter of the rambler-rose trellis. He raised one foot in salute.

"Dear lady!" Crow croaked, ignoring her bedraggled state. He understood that she had suffered a great loss. He was a busybody and had heard about Chipmunk.

"Don't try to explain, Miss Hickory," he said hoarsely. "We all have our troubles. I told you that something would turn up. It has."

"What?" She stood up and leaned against the trellis.

"First of all," he told her, "you must realize that a change, travel, a new scene, are good for all of us. Especially you, Miss Hickory, need a change. You have been living for two years with those who feel that they need a grocery store, a Ford car, a stove, and storm windows. You have grown soft."

She held out her arms, no longer proud.

"Don't preach to me, Crow! What has turned up?"

"A new home for you." He gave a hop-jig step and a swing for show. "Don't ask any questions, but come along with me. There isn't any time to lose. I shall very likely be off for good tomorrow and I want to see you well settled in before I leave. Come with me, dear lady."

Miss Hickory stumbled weakly toward Crow, but he caught her underneath one wide black wing. His wing was like a tent, warm and strong. His big yellow feet guided her small twig ones as the two left the Old Place behind and took to the road. He shortened his steps to suit hers, talking earnestly in his rough voice as he led her toward the orchard.

"You spoke of the untidiness of my nest. How right you are, Miss Hickory. Sticks, chaff and bark are all I ever use. But please realize that I am a man of affairs. I spend my days here and there, in the cornfield, the orchard, the vegetable garden. All I need in the way of a home is a place to hang my hat. But my nest is built high at the top of a tall pine tree as a lookout. From it I saw your new home."

They reached the orchard.

"Turn this way," he told her. "We are going to follow McIntosh Lane along the sidehill. You can't imagine how sheltered it is there, under the lee of the mountain with the pine woods up above for a windbreak. Lean on me, Miss Hickory. We are almost there."

As they found and took the stubble-grown path where the older apple trees had twisted in odd bent shapes, the better to climb the sidehill of the orchard and reach the sun, Miss Hickory felt herself floating, rather than trudging along. She was lifted off her feet every now and then as she clung to Crow's wing. She felt again the energy that the woods always gave her. The exercise of trying to keep up with Crow warmed her. Her heart pounded with excitement, for she believed that Crow was helping her to begin a great adventure. Perhaps a small log cabin with a fireplace and a chimney was waiting on beyond. When she had signed the lease she would return, evict Chipmunk and move her things up there to the sidehill on McIntosh Lane.

"Is it much farther?" she gasped.

Crow was muttering and did not answer at once. He had

never been able to count above one. One cherry; gulp it down. One plump green pea. One mouthful of corn. His father had taught him the Corn-planting Rule:

> "One for the cut-worm
> One for the crow,
> One for the farmer . . ."

"Never mind the rest of it," Crow's father had said. "It signifies nothing for us until later: *'Two to grow.'*"

So Crow was not counting the trees on the side hill, but naming them.

"Cherry. Northern Spy. Clapp's Favorite Pear. McIntosh. McIntosh. Mc—Mc—Tosh—Tosh—." His tongue was becoming twisted. "Here we are!" he told her at last, as they were halfway or so along the sidehill and deep among the leafless gnarled shapes of the apple trees. He stopped beneath one that had not seemed worth pruning that spring. The branches touched the ground and it leaned comfortably toward the slope of the hill, away from the wind. He loosed his hold on Miss Hickory and hopped toward a low-lying bough. "Climb up!" he ordered.

"But— I don't understand." She hesitated.

Crow spread his wings and disappeared among the branches of the apple tree but his voice croaked down to her:

"He who hesitates is lost. Do you or do you not want to live until spring? Climb, I told you!"

She grasped the low bough. How homelike it felt in her strong little twig fingers!

"Swing a bit and then jump!" Crow's call came to her from higher up. This, she decided, was a game that he wanted her to learn. She pulled on the bough, swayed pleasantly a moment and then jumped to another branch farther on.

"Keep on!" Crow croaked. "Climb along up."

So she continued to swing, jump and climb, feeling more adventurous and bold with each step. Up, up, Miss Hickory climbed into the apple tree until the ground was dizzying to look down upon and she could see Temple Mountain, keeping vigil to the West.

"How much farther?" she called.

"Here you are," he answered from a perch right beside her. "Careful now. Easy does it. How's this, dear lady, for your new home?"

She looked in astonishment at what he pointed out to her, a large and deep nest resting securely in a crotch of the apple tree. Crow knew that it might not suit her at first sight so he began to argue and boast, like a real estate agent.

"Light and heat free, whenever the sun shines. A long lease. Although Robin built it for his own use and planned to stay north this winter, Mr. T. Willard-Brown drove him away. Hooks for hanging your clothes; Robin builds carelessly and leaves twigs sticking out. Insulated against the cold with good country mud." Crow's sales talk went on and on, but Miss Hickory had not listened after he had mentioned Mr. T. Willard-Brown. No cat, she decided, would drive *her* out of her home. She balanced on a bough and inspected the empty nest. It was indeed well placed, sheltered and strong. As she peered inside she saw that the wind had cushioned the empty nest deeply with milkweed down and lined it with rose-brown oak leaves. She stepped inside and sank down deliciously into its warm comfort.

"Not bad at all, Crow," she admitted.

"It struck me favorably," he croaked.

The nest was so well suited to her size that when she stood up, she had to stretch a bit to pull herself out. When she lay down, as she now did, for she was very tired, she was snug and unseen. She was alone in a world that had no need of the things she had left behind.

"I don't know what I shall do here all winter," she said, "without a broom in my hands."

"You'll find plenty to do," he told her. "New things to collect, new friends, new places to explore. Well, it's time I was off."

"I am greatly obliged to you, Crow." She leaned over the edge of the nest as Crow opened his wings.

"Don't give it a thought," he said.

"How long until spring?" she ventured to ask. "They took the Old Farmer's Almanac to Boston."

"It doesn't matter," he assured her. "Spring always comes. Remember this, though, dear lady. This is important. Get it through your head. *Keep your sap running!*"

Crow spread his wings, cawed loudly and started. Miss Hickory watched Crow cross the Old Place, the barn, the woods, then disappear as he flew toward the south.

4. SQUIRREL FINDS A LIVE NUT

SQUIRREL had decided that it was high time to begin getting ready for the winter. He had been putting off storing nuts from day to day all autumn because the bright
brisk days were such a delight to him. He liked to scurry
through the fallen leaves in the woods, with their rustling
like dance music to his quick little ears. He loved to scamper
up the trees to a topmost branch, balance on the end of a
bough, swing gaily, then jump to another tree. When these
games were done, he would sit in the sunshine on a stone
wall, frisking and admiring his beautiful tail.

That was what Squirrel was doing one day in late October,
sitting on the stones with the sun shining warm on his back
and his beautiful tail held high like a plume, when he
found the peanut.

It had been left there on the stone wall for Chipmunk, who was now living in luxury in the corncob house underneath the lilac bush, that had once been Miss Hickory's home. Chipmunk was so pleased at having a roof over his head that he seldom visited his old wall. Squirrel held the peanut in his paws. He sniffed it. He rattled it.

"Just what I need for a Sunday dinner next winter," he thought, "I will bury it at once."

But as quickly as his good intention came, it left him. "Too thin a shell to keep," Squirrel decided. "I may not see another peanut until spring." And with that he cracked and ate it.

As soon as Squirrel had enjoyed the peanut, his conscience began to trouble him.

"It is high time that I began to get ready for the winter," he chattered, and off to the woods he scampered where with no difficulty at all he found a sweet ripe beechnut. He was no longer hungry so he dug a deep hole beside the beech tree, buried the nut, and, feeling very pleased with himself, ran a little way through the drifts of leaves with quick dancing steps. But Squirrel had not gone far when his stomach began to feel empty.

"One peanut is nothing for a young man as active as I," he said to himself. "I shall dig up that beechnut for a little snack."

Alas, when Squirrel retraced his footsteps to a beech tree, dug fast and deep at the roots, he could not find his nut. There were many beech trees in the woods, all of them much alike, and Squirrel had forgotten the one beneath which he had buried the nut.

"Very poor memory on my part," he said to himself. "I must try again."

This time Squirrel found a plump acorn, good winter food because of its rich meat. He dug another hole, deeper and close to an oak tree. He buried his acorn and, in order to make no mistake about finding it, he placed a bright red vine beside the hole for a marker. Then Squirrel was off again, climbing trees, waving his beautiful tail and feeling satisfied with himself.

The exercise gave Squirrel an appetite. At the end of an hour he was again hungry. "That one stale peanut was not a meal for me," he repeated to himself. "What I need is a large meaty acorn rich in vitamins."

So Squirrel went back to an oak tree that had a bright red vine at its roots. He dug and dug. He scurried from one spot to another. He excavated here, there; hither and yon. Alas, the woods were full of oak trees with bright red vines trailing on the ground around them. Squirrel had again forgotten where he had buried a nut for his winter store.

Miss Hickory's first thought after she had settled herself in Robin's nest in the apple tree on McIntosh Lane was about new clothes. In spite of her stiff twig body and nut head, Miss Hickory was intensely feminine. Also, she knew that a blue-and-white checked gingham dress and a white cap with ruffles and ties were not suitable for winter wear. She had made another discovery, too, since moving. She had found out that she was not nearly so dependent upon store goods as when she had been living in her corncob house under the lilac bush. She had filled nooks of her nest with wild rose hips, partridgeberries and checkerberries. She had rearranged Robin's carelessly built walls so that she could hang things on the sticks. And she had taught herself how to stitch and tailor with pine needles.

The woods were full of lovely stuffs for her sewing. Velvety leaves not yet dried and colored rose, gold, scarlet and russet. Soft beautiful mosses of many different kinds: furry ones, that grew close to the ground; trailing ones; upstanding feathery ones like plumes. And each moss was green and everlasting. The tiny brown cones of the larch trees made excellent buttons. The soft lining of the fern fronds made Miss Hickory's winter underwear. She spent many happy hours alone and busy in the woods, selecting materials, and sitting on a toadstool sewing. The winter wardrobe she designed and fitted to herself was a model of style and utility. Since she had become so like the woods in her dress and habits she was almost invisible as she took her way among the evergreens and the falling leaves. That was why Squirrel did not see her. He was so confused at forgetting where he had buried his nuts that he was talking to himself.

"Nutty, in the broader sense of the word!" Squirrel said aloud. "That seems to be growing on me!"

"So I have noticed."

Squirrel jumped. The voice was sharp and elderly. But

when he found courage to follow the voice he came to a small person sitting on a toadstool, her feet in their bark shoes swinging and her dress gay enough for going to a party. She looked blithe and young, due to her costume. But Miss Hickory's sharp nose was even sharper and her black eyes were piercing.

She wore a dress of layer upon layer of golden beech leaves. Her coat was made of short, low-growing moss, thick and warm, with tiny larch cones for buttons and a border of creeping pine. Her close-fitting hat was little more than a cap, but smart. It matched her coat, being made of green moss, and it had a bunch of red-alder berries and one moss plume for trimming. She had made herself a little round muff of a scarlet maple leaf and lined it with fern down. She looked years younger. Squirrel thought her enchanting.

"Hi, cutie!" he greeted her.

"Mind your manners, my lad!" Miss Hickory warned him. "I have been watching you for some time. I don't approve of your scatterbrained ways. You seem to have a very poor memory."

"How true! I was spoiled as a child," he told her sadly. "An only child, who had all the nuts I wanted given me. I was not a strong child either." Squirrel wiped an imaginary tear from his eye with one gray paw.

At the word *nuts* Miss Hickory started. She pulled her hat down lower to hide the shape of her head. She got down from the toadstool and backed into a thicket of young hemlock shoots.

"Excuses! Nothing but a tall story!" she called shrilly. "You are one of a large family. I know, for I watched you growing up. Your mother taught you to hide nuts—" She stopped, covering her mouth with her muff. *Nut*. The one word she should have avoided.

Squirrel Finds a Live Nut

Squirrel's ears rose. He came closer to Miss Hickory and peered into her face. She could not turn her head away from him. Squirrel sniffed her. He tapped her nose playfully.

"A nut! That's what you think I am?" he chattered. "How about you? Where did you get your head?"

She turned and hurried away, but Squirrel followed her. She could run fast but he leaped. Over stubble and stones, out of the woods and through the jungle of dry sumac bushes he pursued her. Miss Hickory climbed the stone wall into the orchard, but Squirrel jumped over it and was waiting for her on the other side. Squirrel's sharp white teeth showed in a grin as they came to McIntosh Lane but, surprisingly, he did not touch her. As a matter of fact all Squirrel wanted was a race.

Up her apple tree Miss Hickory scrambled. She dashed into her nest, looking over the edge fearfully. Squirrel was down below, on the ground.

"Hickory, Miss Hickory, is my name," she called to him, trying to awe Squirrel and saying exactly what she had not intended to divulge.

"So I thought when I saw your head!" he replied. "Such a good race, was it not? There's nothing like a cross-country run on a frosty morning for getting one home in time for dinner."

"Home!" she gasped.

"Why, yes. Quite a coincidence, Miss Hickory," Squirrel chattered on. "I have my hole right here, at the foot of your tree. My mother left it to me in her will."

5. MISS HICKORY'S GOOD DEED

HEN-PHEASANT and Miss Hickory left the brush pile in the pine wood. Side by side they crossed the orchard, turned into the field called High-Mowing, and walked toward the wild lot across from the Old Place where blueberries grew.

"Cock is away on business?" Miss Hickory asked. "I saw him coming along this way early."

Hen-Pheasant, a drab little creature with neither color nor liveliness, gave a mournful cluck.

"Now, in November, Cock has left me," she told Miss Hickory. "He has moved to the other side of the brush pile. He does not let me have any breakfast."

"Is that the custom?" Miss Hickory asked. Looking at Hen-Pheasant, she saw that here was no glamorous creature like Cock-Pheasant, who walked in grandeur, his tail feathers trailing like ribbons of rainbow.

"He left me last autumn too," Hen-Pheasant said. "He began to neglect me about this time. Every morning when I walked behind Cock at a respectful distance, when we came to a feeding place he turned and pecked me home again."

"Brutal! No gentleman!" Miss Hickory stamped her foot. "What did you do about it, Hen?"

"Nothing!" she answered dolefully.

There seemed to be little left to say so they went on side by side in silence. Miss Hickory, since she had found out that Squirrel lived at the roots of her apple tree on McIntosh Lane, had stayed away from her nest as much as possible. Squirrel had not molested her, but she valued her head too highly to take any risks. One evening when she had hung up her hat and undressed, had settled within her downy bed and covered herself, she was startled to see two bright eyes peering at her. Squirrel had climbed up and was looking over the rim of her nest. But he came no farther.

"Just came up to be neighborly," he chattered. "Pleasant dreams!" Then he was gone.

Pleasant dreams indeed! Miss Hickory had put on her hat and pulled it down tightly. She had not slept a wink. And ever since that night she had worn her hat to bed.

So now, in November, she was down the tree and about every day, enjoying the autumn leaves. They enfolded her in color. They lay beneath her feet, blowing on their merry stems to keep her company. They spread a carpet of russet, gold and scarlet upon the mountain. Miss Hickory saw new colors each day as the mountain changed from the flames of the maples to the rosy glow of the turning oaks. She was never cold, for her sap was running well. She thought it silly that Hen-Pheasant should feel sorry for herself at so bright a season of the year. Hen-Pheasant trudged silently along, her head low. Miss Hickory turned on her at last.

"If I were in your place, Hen, I wouldn't allow it," she scolded. "I should teach him to be a gentleman."

"How?" Hen asked mildly. "That is the custom among the cocks. Some autumns they allow us to have breakfast with them. Sometimes not. Are you a schoolteacher?" she asked curiously.

"I plan to take over a school next spring." The idea had just popped into Miss Hickory's head.

"Then you have brains. Perhaps you can advise me."

As a matter of fact, Miss Hickory could think of no means of teaching Cock-Pheasant good manners. But just then they came upon a surprise. They came suddenly upon a shelter for wintering birds where High-Mowing ended and the blueberry pasture began. The mower would have been called slack by anyone who did not understand him. In truth he was very kind. He had allowed the tall grasses and the weeds to grow high where a stone wall make a wind-break. There were some ears of corn left standing there also, for food. It was a better winter home for little Hen-Pheasant than the rough brush pile in the woods. Miss Hickory clapped her hands.

"Look, Hen," she shrilled, "something has turned up."

Hen-Pheasant stepped into the shelter and pecked at a few kernels of corn. But her small gray head still drooped and her feathers hung, draggled and slack. Miss Hickory lost patience.

"Hold your head up, Hen! Here you are in a winter shelter with seeds and corn on your doorstep, and you droop. Hold your head up, I say, and be thankful."

"I won't be allowed to stay here," Hen-Pheasant sighed, her head still lower. "Cock will cluck me out."

That, Miss Hickory saw, was exactly what might happen. Cock-Pheasant would come along, along over the snow, his feathers splashing a line of gold and scarlet against the white. He would come upon the shelter beside the stone wall, with the stalks of corn and the grasses that the mower had left. He would drive Hen out and move in himself. The situation seemed hopeless. Miss Hickory thought hard-headedly. She drew upon her past.

"Hen," she said at last, "are there other hens in the same difficulty as you?"

"All of us. Our cocks refuse to nest with us in the winter.

They live together in their club on the other side of the brush pile until spring."

"Then," Miss Hickory told her, "you must do the same. You must all make yourselves comfortable until spring right here. If you take a stand, no cock will dare to drive you out. You must form a Ladies' Aid Society."

"How? I don't know what you mean." But Hen-Pheasant raised her dull little eyes to Miss Hickory's snapping ones.

"Easy enough! The first thing that the Ladies' Aid Society of Hillsborough does every autumn is to start making a bed quilt. They sew together pretty pieces of cloth that they have gathered and saved, flowery pieces, plain pieces, but al' colored. They meet at the Town Hall once a week to make their patched squares into one large quilt of many colors. Then they line it, stuff it, and quilt it on a frame. They sell their quilt in the spring at a church fair. But you, Hen, might as well keep yours and use it this winter."

Hen-Pheasant's slow-working mind reeled. Not a word of Miss Hickory's good idea had she understood.

"Sew! Patches! Ladies' Aid!" she mumbled.

"Yes." Miss Hickory hurried over to the edge of the woods and was gone for a few moments. She returned with some sharp green pine needles and four straight and slender branches for a quilting frame. She then gathered four beautiful fallen leaves. A russet oak leaf, a yellow beech leaf, a red maple leaf, and a golden maple leaf. She laid them together in a pattern of patchwork before Hen-Pheasant and showed her how to sew them together with a pine needle

and a thread of dried grass. It pleased Hen-Pheasant. She took a pine needle in one claw and began stitching the patch of leaves. Sewing seemed to come to her naturally.

"Look up at the mountain," Miss Hickory said, "for your pattern and colors, and your quilt will be the only one of its kind. The ladies of the Ladies' Aid Society make patched quilts indoors. They also have a colored mountain to look at, but they like to make their own pattern."

Hen-Pheasant looked up at Temple Mountain shining in the sun, glowing with its autumn leaves. Scarlet sumac at the foot. Green pines on top. Layer on layer of the bright oaks and maples between. She had never looked at it before, having always felt sorry for herself when the leaves began to turn. Even to glance at that beauty brightened her.

"Now, here," Miss Hickory went on working briskly, "is your quilting frame." She tied the four branches together with strong grasses to make a square frame. "When you finish the patches and sew them together to make your quilt, tie it on this frame and sew it up and down, back and forth; that is called quilting. And, oh, I forgot to tell you. The other thing that the Ladies' Aid Society does is to eat. They have a big dinner on the days when they meet in the Town Hall to work on their quilt—"

But Hen-Pheasant scarcely heard her. She had gathered herself a pile of corn over which she was clucking, singing a little tune of happiness, stitching a patch of leaves, pecking a kernel or two now and then. Miss Hickory went softly away. Hen-Pheasant did not see her go.

"She's all right now, safe for the winter. I will stop at the brush pile and tell the other hens where they may join her. I will explain to them about the Ladies' Aid Society."

Miss Hickory felt rather like a Boy Scout as she walked briskly toward the woods.

6. BARN NEWS

COW HAD been gone from the barn all day, and Mr. T. Willard-Brown was anxious about her. Not on Cow's account. Oh, no! He had only cupboard love for Cow and had missed his daily saucer of warm milk. As he sat beside a mousehole in the barn, Mr. T. Willard-Brown's mind wandered. He remembered the day last summer when Cow had been away also, that time for a day and a night.

It had been a day last summer when anyone would have wished to be away from the barn. The three brooks that flowed through the Old Place's acres and emptied into the pond had been gurgling all the tunes they knew. Young corn was bursting into ears. Baby birds were trying their wings over the sunny grass of High-Mowing. Cow seldom gave heed to the beauties of nature, but that day she had felt a strong urge to get away from stalls and milking pails. She had stepped slowly over the barn threshold and taken her way heavily down the road, past High-Mowing, and then along First Brook into the woods. She had drunk deeply of the sweet, cool water. Then, where some young white birches made a sheltered spinney carpeted with moss and dimly secret, Cow had lain down. That was a luxury which she seldom allowed herself. There in the hidden spinney Cow had rested, her big heart warm.

The morning of the second day Mr. T. Willard-Brown could endure his thirst no longer. He had started out to find Cow. No one in the barn seemed to share his concern about Cow, so he traveled alone. He had crept through the tall grasses of Acre-Piece, followed the stone wall that marked High-Mowing, and then, fancying that his nose scented milk, he trailed into the woods. There, still resting on the velvet moss of the birch spinney, Mr. T. Willard-Brown had found Cow.

But Cow was not alone. On either side of her great brown haunches lay a young heifer. Cow turned from side to side, her brown eyes full of love, licking first one small soft daughter with her rough tongue, then licking the other. Two newborn heifers! Mr. T. Willard-Brown stopped dead in his tracks. Twins! That was unusual. No cow in all Hillsborough had ever given birth to twins. As he looked at the twin heifers, mottled-brown like Cow, their eyes as wide and hazel as hers, the three saw him. Cow arose lumberingly. The heifers, too, found that their spindly legs would hold them and they stood, leaning against their mother.

"This way," Mr. T. Willard-Brown told them. Waving his long tail that quivered with excitement even to its white tip, he led Cow and Twin-Heifers out of the woods and toward the barn.

Now, in November, Twin-Heifers were able to take care of themselves. Their big eyes were as dark as Third Brook when brown oak leaves floated on the surface. Their brindled coats were still soft, but the hair had grown in thicker for winter warmth. Their slender legs were strong. But the twins, to the surprise of Cow and the entire barn as well, were alike only in appearance. In their manners and tastes they could hardly have been recognized as sisters. Barn-Heifer was home-loving, sober and polite. She knew that she belonged in the barn, that the barnyard was her front yard and that she should come in to supper promptly. Her bedtime found her in the soft straw of Cow's stall and the crooning of the hens on their perches sang her to sleep.

But not her sister! Ah, no!

There were forest strains in Wild-Heifer's blood. She felt choked by the barn walls. Tied to a post in the barnyard, Wild-Heifer pulled it up and was off, dragging post and rope behind her. She often missed her supper, seeming to thrive on stubble and gleanings. She was sometimes out all night.

Wild-Heifer was gone from the barn that day, and Mr. T.

Willard-Brown finally left his mousehole and crossed the flooring stealthily. He would, he decided, hide behind the opened door and find out when Wild-Heifer came home. When Cow, who was probably out hunting for her wandering daughter, returned, Mr. T. Willard-Brown would tattle. But even he, used to the ways of the country and not easily shocked, felt his neck hairs rising and his tail becoming large as toward evening he saw Cow coming down the road.

Ever since the birth of Twin-Heifers Cow had felt herself superior. She had felt that even giving the usual amount of milk was not necessary. Her picture, together with that of her daughters, had been in the Hillsborough News with a printed piece about them. Cow had decided that now her time had come for a life of pleasure. As Cow would have put it, she could rest on her laurels. And this, in fact, was just what Cow had been doing that day, resting among laurel bushes and stuffing herself with windfall apples where a pile of them had been dumped under the lee of Temple Mountain. But first, as she had started out on her adventure that morning, Cow had stopped in the truck garden and eaten a whole winter squash. It was an acorn squash, with a hard green shell and richly yellow inside. She had eaten the acorn squash shell and all. Then, on a morning breeze, Cow had got a whiff of the rotting apples. It had been beyond her power to resist. When she had eaten more of the apples than was wise, Cow had arisen with difficulty from her bed of laurels, staggered down to the road and started home.

Mr. T. Willard-Brown's tail had reason to become large

at the sight of Cow. She had lost all sense of respectability. She was not walking, but jigging her way home, doing a poor kind of tap dance from one side of the road to the other past the Acre-Piece, by High-Mowing, trying at last to get through the barnyard gate. She felt that it had been a successful day. As she came capering along, Cow gave deep-throated *moos* of satisfaction. One could understand from Cow's behavior, Mr. T. Willard-Brown thought, how Wild-Heifer had come by her wildness. He ran out to the gate to point out the gateposts between which Cow must enter. She made it, but inside the barn she collapsed. As happens often when one eats too much, Cow had a tremendous stomach-ache. Her *moos* changed from hilarity to calls for help.

Mr. T. Willard-Brown ran mewing for the farmer. Cow needed medicine, and as he had seen her being dosed in the

past he knew how exciting the sight would be. If Cow had been able to swallow in a civilized way like the horses and the sheep, her medicine would have gone down easily. But since Cow ordinarily lived on cuds, chewing them for long periods of time, and had a special digestive system, she swallowed differently from most animals. She had to be stood on her back legs against the side of her stall, which was an uncomfortable and undignified stance, to have a dose of medicine poured down her throat.

As the farmer started toward the barn with a bottle, Mr. T. Willard-Brown decided to let Miss Hickory see the performance. Although he had heard where she was living he had not as yet called upon her. He remembered her sharp remarks just before she had moved, but he was not a man to treasure his hurt feelings. So Mr. T. Willard-Brown raced up to the orchard, along McIntosh Lane, and climbed the tree where Miss Hickory had her nest.

Miss Hickory had gone to bed early. She liked to lie snug and warm as she watched the setting sun turn the leaves on the mountainside into a curtain of jewels. Then, in an apple-green sky, cold and cloudless, the sun would set. Miss Hickory would pull her hat down as far as she could and say a small prayer, asking that she might find her head still on when she awoke. So it was not surprising that she was terrified to see Mr. T. Willard-Brown's eyes, like headlights, peering at her over the rim of her nest.

"Come over with me to the barn, Miss Hickory," Mr. T. Willard-Brown purred. "Cow is going to be given medicine. She has a stomach-ache."

"Is that all you have to say for yourself? Must you rouse me from my beauty sleep with such a poor excuse? What is it that you really want, Tippy?"

"Only to give you a few moments of entertainment," he said sadly. "You'll be sorry if you do not come over, Miss Hickory. This is going to be good." He climbed down the tree, purring back through the branches.

"You have probably not heard the barn news. One of Cow's twins has turned out badly. She runs away. You would best watch your step, Miss Hickory. Wild-Heifer is often in the orchard and might easily mistake you for a little green bush with red berries. Do you want to be eaten, Miss Hickory?"

That, he felt, was a proper retort. He padded home as fast as he could. But Miss Hickory did not move.

7. RUNAWAY FAWN

THE FIRST lesson that Fawn learned was the lay of the land. Doe, his mother, taught him. He seldom saw the great antlered buck, his father, but Doe was by Fawn's side from sunrise until sunset. And he slept beside her in the old lost cellar hole that was their home, close to her soft brown coat for warmth.

Fawn was newborn that season, a dappled deer creature with hoofs like fairy feet and eyes that were hazel brown and caught and held the sunlight. His eyes could hold tears though, if Doe left him in the deep grass or among soft bushes. She ran alone once in a while to teach him to take care of himself.

The cellar hole that had once held a home had been

abandoned for many years. None but a dweller of the forest could have found it, for its road was lost, its stones were overgrown with wild brier and sumac, and the old gray birches that had sprouted around it were now tall and arched by the winds into a roof. But the cellar hole could remember. There, on one side, a brick fireplace had once stood with the bean pot snugly simmering in its oven, the andirons holding four-foot logs, and a mother rocking a cradle and knitting on the wide hearth. The cellar hole remembered spinning wheels and sleigh bells, sizzling doughnuts and molasses cookies, fishing tackle, guns, singing school and Bible readings, hardships and laughter, snowdrifts and white lilacs. Now it was nothing but an ancient memory-book of things past. The thicket of black alder, pine and hemlock that led to it kept its pages closed to all except those who love the country. And when Doe had been searching for a safe home for her fallow deer, the cellar hole had seemed right. There was not even a footpath where the long-lost road had led to its smoking chimney. Granite rocks covered with lichen and moss were the only sign posts. Lying within the shelter of the cellar hole, Doe licked Fawn with her caressing tongue and the wind among the pine trees sang him to sleep.

"Where the road begins is East," Doe told Fawn. "Next spring when your legs are fleeter you may go that way for an adventure. There are gardens with peas and beans to nibble, young fruit trees with sweet bark, pears and cherries lying on the ground, and rosebuds to nibble for your dessert. Once I looked in through a kitchen window. I saw pumpkin pies on the table, but that is not a safe trip for you yet. East is where the sun rises. When you run East, remember that your hoofprints are plainly to be seen."

Then Doe spoke of the West.

"The road home, toward the woods and the sunset, lies West. We pass the barn at the North and follow the Acre-Piece close to the woods. There are a few ancient and neglected apple trees within its walls. We shall find the buds on the Acre-Piece apple trees good eating. On the other side of the road is the orchard where the Gravensteins, the Winesaps, the Northern Spies, the Baldwins and the McIntoshes climb the hill. Avoid the orchard!" Doe warned him.

"Don't run South," she advised. "None of our family run that way. Only birds go South in the winter."

"The North—" Doe lifted her great dark eyes in a daydream. "Your father came from the North. He came to me from the forests of the North, swimming the mountain streams, with trailing waterweeds and vines streaming from his antlers. He came with the Herd, homing for the winter. The others went up the side of the mountain, but your father stayed here in the valley with me."

"Where is he now?" Fawn asked, pawing the earth in impatience to be trailing.

"I have not seen your father since the hunting season began. Listen! Mark my words! Stay close to home until the snow drifts. If you hear a loud noise, or a crackling in the bushes—"

But Fawn could endure his mother's lessons no longer. He raised his small pointed ears to catch the good scents of the forest. He poised a moment, like a bird ready for flight. Then he was off, swift and carefree. Tiny hoofmarks in the fresh light snow, close together as he ran, then far apart as he leaped, so Fawn left his trail away from the cellar hole. He was spotted tan and white like the moving shadows of the woods, and thus invisible. He was so young and so fleet that adventure was all that impelled him.

"Off to the East!" Fawn thought. "I must look in that kitchen window."

Out of the forest on winged hoofs, leaping stone walls, trailing close to the brown tree trunks that hid him, Fawn crossed the Acre-Piece, passed the barn, and came to the garden of the Old Place. All was still. There were no footprints on the white page of new snow. Fawn stepped

delicately up the back steps, put his front feet on the windowsill and tried to peep into the kitchen. Alas, the curtains were drawn. He could not see a single pie, as he had hoped to do. And suddenly a rustling in the bare lilac bushes at the back of the house startled Fawn. He saw a little house built of corncobs that stood beneath the lilac bush. It seemed deserted. No smoke rose from the chimney and small snow drifts covered the windows. Fawn bravely came closer to the corncob house, sniffing it delicately. But a tiny pointed red face appeared at the door, then a striped coat and a furiously waving tail. Chipmunk chattered *no trespassers*, and with beating heart and flying feet Fawn was off toward the orchard.

He found tasty roots and bark to eat in the orchard. He nuzzled through the snow and the thick blanket of grasses and leaves deep into the warm ground where berries and juicy vine leaves waited. Eating, sniffing the rich soil, raising his head to feel the falling stars of snow, Fawn felt quite safe and very happy, with new strength in his limbs. Now and then his head felt ticklish as if with a hint of sprouting antlers. He would, he thought, explain to Doe that he was growing up fast. He could and would run alone, returning to her, of course, at night.

Crash, Bang! The quiet air was broken into echoes of terror. A gun! Fawn had heard the hunter's gun before. He suddenly realized that he was alone. He leaped here, there, in panic as he tried to remember the way home. He bounded down through the orchard, crossed the road, and stood unprotected for a space in the Acre-Piece trying to remember where the West lay. The sun was high, no help at all in showing him where it would set. But presently as Fawn looked down he saw what seemed to be a bright round red berry lying at his feet on top of the snow. But was it that? As Fawn dipped his little pointed nose toward the red berry it disappeared, and when he pawed away the snow he came upon nothing but stubble. It was a mystery. He discovered more of the round red spots in the snow of the Acre-Piece and followed them until they led him to the edge of the forest. Each was gone as if it had been a gleam of will-of-the-wisp fire as Fawn touched it with nose or hoof.

He had forgotten the crash of the gun as he found his way home, following the crimson trail into the woods, so familiar and safe. He hardly noticed that the red spots on the snow drew a line of red as he followed them. The first snow was so light that it had not yet covered the floor of the forest. Fawn had no difficulty at last in finding the cellar hole. He had a great deal to tell his mother; how he had looked in a window, how he had seen a chipmunk who lived in a little corncob house, how Doe knew best about staying close to home during the hunting season. He gave one happy leap into the old cellar hole, but it was empty. And although Fawn looked for Doe until sunset, blind with the tears in his great dark eyes, he did not find her. At last, when the forest was too dark to trail, Fawn understood that Doe must have been looking for him, following him, watching over him, when he had heard the crashing gunfire. He came back and lay down in their cellar hole, cold, shaking with sorrow and fear, all alone.

Fawn thought that he was dreaming when he felt a soft warm flank pressing close beside him. He was in a troubled sleep, light and fitful, because it was one of the first nights of bitter cold. He turned, nuzzled Doe in his dream, and then leaped away as a strange *moo* broke the dark silence. Leaping out of the cellar hole, Fawn saw a creature not so different from himself. A bit plumper, but as softly brown, with big tender eyes, and matching Fawn's height. The strange bedfellow came over and rubbed noses with him. Then it leaned in warm friendliness against Fawn's trembling body. It coaxed Fawn gently into a spinney of birch trees close by where they lay down side by side, and Fawn went to sleep in peace.

So neither was alone again. Wild-Heifer had found a brother, and Fawn a sister. And Wild-Heifer and Fawn ran together after that.

8. WILD-HEIFER'S SUPPER PARTY

CRACK. *Crack! Chatter-chee.* Silence. *Crack-crack!*

Miss Hickory wrinkled her small nut face. Only too well did she know the meaning of those sounds. Down in his hole at the foot of her tree, Squirrel was cracking and eating the nuts that he had harvested at such thought and urging on her part.

Now, in December, with snow on the ground and often a light crust on top of the snow, it was high time to think seriously about food for the winter. Miss Hickory had not completely lost her fear of Squirrel. When they met in the orchard, Squirrel had an uncomfortable way of looking hard, without speaking, at her head. In playful moods, he still tried to pull off her winter hat. In fact, he had taken off and eaten the trimming. But on one of the first stormy nights of the winter when snow fell and their tree rocked with the wind, when Miss Hickory had thought that the snow was an enemy instead of a blanket, Squirrel had come up-boughs. As Miss Hickory pulled her leaf covers up to her chin, shivering more from fear than cold, she had seen two

little gray paws clutching the edge of her nest, two bright eyes peeping in at her. She had sat up in bed.

"And what do you want at this time of night?" she had demanded.

"Only to keep you from worrying, Miss Hickory," Squirrel had said. He came farther and squeezed in beside her, all but his bushy tail that hung outside the nest. "Only to try and keep you warm." Squirrel had patted Miss Hickory's cheek with one paw.

"Very kind of you. *Very* kind, I must say," she had retorted bitterly. "Would you like my bed for the night and let me sleep in your hole? I dare say it is more weather-tight than this nest."

"Oh, no! Thank you so much." Squirrel had scampered down the tree to his cozy hole that was carpeted with old moss and had a pile of nuts in one corner.

"No harm meant," he chattered on his way down.

As she remembered that night, Miss Hickory asked herself if she had been fair to Squirrel. His poor memory, his inability to make a plan, were unfortunate. Yet he had not seemed covetous of her head, only amused at it. So on this day of early winter, Miss Hickory jumped and swung herself down the tree, down-boughs, and stood quite a while at the entrance to Squirrel's hole, only watching. Presently as Squirrel cracked and ate another nut, she spoke.

"How about tomorrow, young lad?" she asked.

Squirrel jumped. He thought hard, trying to find an excuse. Then—"I'll start right out today, gathering more beechnuts," he chattered.

"And then what? Can you remember where your hole is? Can you keep from eating your nuts on the way home? If you do replenish your pantry, will you hold to three meals a day instead of six?"

"Now, Miss Hickory!" Squirrel's bright eyes took on a canny glint. "It is easy for you to keep *your* nut."

Miss Hickory did not wait. She was off and away as fast as her skates would take her. They had been shoes made of strong bark last summer, but rough going and climbing up and down her tree since she moved had worn them to sharp edges. Miss Hickory now had skates or snowshoes, whichever she needed. She skimmed off on the icy crust of the snow as fleet as a deer, and suddenly as happy as a sharp snowy winter day can make one. Her objective was food. No longer could she depend upon her canning of a season ago. But she knew that frozen foods had become popular. Every berrybush and seed pod was her cafeteria. She skated first over the field known as High-Mowing. Black-alder berries grew along the edge; tasty and crisp for a snack. Before she reached their winter shelter, she heard the clucking songs of content that came from the Ladies' Aid Society which she had helped to found. Hen-Pheasant was there, and huddled close beside her were a number of other drab little hens. The blanket of snow that covered the beautiful bed quilt or leaves that they had made only kept them warmer and the colors of the quilt brighter. They seemed happy enough, nesting together without Cock-Pheasant and his lordly fellows. Miss Hickory caught scraps of talk.

"Cock has to walk in his best coattails in plain sight down the road, and into the stubble to get his breakfast. Our food is right here." Hen-Pheasant gave a gay peck at a kernel of corn.

"They'll all come back to us later."

"It is the custom that we and our cocks should nest separately in the winter."

"Plenty of corn and seeds for us right here!"

So the Ladies' Aid Society crooned and clucked.

"They are all right. I won't disturb them," Miss Hickory

thought, as she bit a red-alder berry, then skated across the road and into the Acre-Piece.

First Brook ran along one side of Acre-Piece. Wild roses grew on its banks. Now, in December, there were no leaves on the wild rose bushes but the rose hips covered it with color. Round and painted by the frost, the hips of the wild roses looked like little oranges waiting for Miss Hickory to pick them. She did. *M-m-m*, she said as she crunched the frozen goodness of the fruit and the seeds. Then Miss Hickory rested awhile, looking down, listening to the tiny sound of the brook under its thin roof of ice. She wondered where the brook was going, for it never stood still as the frog pond did. Where did it come from? First Brook had another attraction for Miss Hickory. In summer wild grapes grew on the vines along the banks. Young trees, tall ferns and a tangle of sumac hid the dark purple clusters of the grapes

so that only wood creatures picked them when they ripened in the autumn. There were still many frozen grapes for Miss Hickory's desserts. She cut figure eights on the ice, ate grapes, skimmed on and on along First Brook with the current curling on, on, beneath the ice. She went farther than she knew. All at once the bank looked oddly like old times. She left the ice, climbed the steep bank of First Brook, and there she was at the Old Place! She was just behind the barn.

The hours had slipped by so pleasantly, skating, sliding, eating, that it was nearly suppertime when Miss Hickory reached the barn. The days were short and the sun was setting, a ball of fire in the coldly green West. Miss Hickory remembered Mr. T. Willard-Brown's warning about Wild-Heifer's appetite. She also remembered that she had missed seeing Cow take her medicine after having eaten too much. The barn, Miss Hickory knew, was a warm and friendly place, a shelter for hens and sheep, horses and pigeons, Cow and her twin heifers, as well as for Mr. T. Willard-Brown.

"I should have come over here when he invited me," she said to herself. "Utter pettishness that I didn't."

Just then the barn door opened slightly to let in supper. Corn for the fowls. Mash for the lambs. Hay and oats were pulled down. Miss Hickory was of a mind to slip in through the door, only to warm herself before going home, but she just escaped a galloping heifer dashing in.

"A close call for you, Miss Hickory," Mr. T. Willard-Brown purred into her ear. He had crept up silently, his eyes gleaming like little green traffic lights. "Use my cathole if you want to come inside. You are just in time to see something good, most unusual."

The cathole, small and square, had a hinged door close to the ground. Mr. T. Willard-Brown bumped the door up with his nose, entered the barn, and Miss Hickory followed him, Inside, the hour of good eating filled the barn with content. But Miss Hickory stared in astonishment. The twin heifers were not having their supper in Cow's stall. Only one of the twins, Barn-Heifer, stood quietly eating beside her mother.

Mr. T. Willard-Brown's eyes lighted the dusk as he led Miss Hickory toward the half-opened door. There, eating side by side, stood Wild-Heifer and Fawn. All day they had run together, Wild-Heifer tasting freedom, Fawn sharing his forest secrets. They had grown tall since summer, but could still be taken for sister and brother. Wild-Heifer's legs had learned a swiftness that no other heifer had known. Fawn's dappled coat was losing its spots in his thicker winter one. At first, Fawn had feared the barn. He had waited at suppertime at the woods side of the spinney where four white birch trees made an entrance to the Acre-Piece, with the afterglow of the sunset behind. But Wild-Heifer had urged Fawn to follow her. At last, stepping on winged feet, hesitating with dilated nostrils and raised head, ready to retreat in great arched bounds, Fawn had come to the barn. The pail of good mash waited near the opened door.

"I told you we have strange goings-on here in the barn," Mr. T. Willard-Brown said as he and Miss Hickory watched. "Every night Wild-Heifer shares her supper with Fawn."

9. NOW CHRISTMAS COMES

Now, THE day before Christmas, Miss Hickory felt that something of portent was in the air. Not a feeling that could be put into words, or even worked out in her mind. Nothing was changed, but the fields and the forest seemed expectant. Snow lay deep, but it was criss-crossed and mapped by the imprint of small hurrying feet, rabbits, winter birds and deer. The laurel, whose secret hopes keep it green and fresh all winter, pushed up through the snow asking to be made into Christmas wreaths. The long green fingers of the pine tree held little snowballs, trimming itself for Christmas. Small straight hemlock and spruce trees crowded one another begging to be Christmas trees. Scarlet winter berries blended with the laurel to help in making the Christmas wreaths. And the creeping pine lay bright underneath the snow for twining into garlands.

Miss Hickory remembered last Christmas. She had lived then on the kitchen windowsill of the Old Place. There, she had sniffed mince pies, turkey and Christmas pudding, the Christmas tree in the parlor, and boiling molasses taffy. She had been given a tiny green hemlock shoot as a Christmas tree for her corncob house, and a new little gingham apron. But her life was so changed now that last Christmas was only the dimmest memory. She skated and coasted about her pleasant winter world, nibbling bark and rose hips, sticking a laurel leaf in her hat to replace the trimming Squirrel had tweaked off, and giving little thought, since she had no Old Farmer's Almanac, to the season.

That was why Miss Hickory did not believe Squirrel. He dashed up-boughs to her nest as it began to be dusk. "Full moon tonight, Miss Hickory," he announced. "Bright moonlight for Christmas Eve. You mustn't go to bed too early. Stay up for the celebration."

"What celebration?" Miss Hickory pulled her hat down tightly. Even now, after so many weeks, she did not really trust Squirrel.

"In the barn," he told her. "Something wonderful happens there every Christmas Eve at midnight. My mother took me over last Christmas to see it. Only we animals and the winged creatures see it. Large and small, wild and tame, of the earth or with God, we all go over to the barn to watch for it, and no one is afraid of those larger than himself."

Miss Hickory

"I have outgrown bedtime stories," Miss Hickory said crossly as she tucked her covers close about her feet. "You go, Squirrel, if you believe all this nonsense."

"The wonder on Christmas Eve is this," Squirrel continued, not noticing her remark. "In one of the barn mangers, the animal to whom it belongs finds the wonder. In the fresh grain of his manger, at midnight tonight, there will be a small hollow, although the straw and oats were freshly laid and not touched. It will be the shape of a baby's head and body. Do you know what a baby is, Miss Hickory?" he asked anxiously.

"I have seen them, but never in a barn in the dead of winter," she said sharply. "Nor have you," she snapped.

"I assure you that I saw Christmas Eve in the barn." Squirrel wrinkled his little gray forehead, sorry not to be believed.

"Just a dream that you had last night after eating too many nuts. Oh, I hear you day after day, night after night, cracking, eating." But he would not be silenced.

"Then all the animals, the barn creatures and the wild creatures, see the wonder too. They crowd around the manger and—"

"Posh!" said Miss Hickory. "I have heard enough of your fancy talk. Get down-boughs, home!"

"You'll be sorry." Squirrel felt that he had been insulted. He rapped Miss Hickory's head so hard with a paw that her hat went askew. "Hardheaded!" he said as he left her.

That was coming to be a familiar description of her, Miss Hickory thought. But the fact that she had a nut for a head did make new ideas difficult for her mind to grasp. She was coming to realize that fact.

"I'll have a good night's rest and go over to the barn in the morning," she thought. "Then I can see whatever there is to see."

So on Christmas Eve Miss Hickory went to sleep early and she slept soundly until a loud sweet chiming awoke her. Like elfin bells the frosted twigs and icicles that covered her tree clashed and tinkled and rang out merry tunes. As her tree chimed, all the other trees joined in the chorus until the orchard shook and thrilled with carols. Miss Hickory sat up in bed, and the Christmas Eve moonlight on the snow was so dazzling that she rubbed her eyes, got out of bed, and went farther up-boughs to see what it was all about. As soon as she reached the top she understood that something extraordinary was taking place.

Down from the peak of Temple Mountain, into its lee and passing through the orchard in the direction of the barn, Miss Hickory saw a strange procession. Flying ahead like a courier came a crow, but not Crow whom Miss Hickory knew, for this one was white. Following the white crow came the robins with sprays of holly in their bills and the bluebirds carrying laurel leaves. Fawn came next, but to Miss Hickory's surprise Doe, his mother, was beside him again. The two, Fawn and Doe, stepped lightly and in time to the orchard chimes. They came slowly, looking neither toward the woods or the fields, for they were not afraid.

Miss Hickory chuckled when she saw Cock-Pheasant, a

brilliant painting as his beautiful tail feathers trailed the snow. He joined the Christmas parade at High-Mowing, where he had called at the headquarters of the Ladies' Aid Society for Hen-Pheasant. She walked in the procession at a respectful distance behind Cock. But Miss Hickory held her breath as the peacocks came in handsome array down the mountainside, tails of jeweled color or white lace spread in great fans. Nightingales came singing; green and gold parrots flew past in pairs with palm leaves in their bills; light-footed goats with bells at their throats danced. When she saw the camels marching, tall and majestic in silk trappings, she was frightened. But the home creatures who mingled fearlessly among these others from far away seemed not at all afraid. A white skunk and her family went by, the wood-chucks who had come out of their holes for this occasion, and hosts of scampering rabbits and herds of deer. Owls left their holes. The blind moles seemed to have their sight. The large ones in the procession stepped carefully so as not to harm the small ones. Field mice came tripping along the snow leaving their footprints in a white pattern of dance steps. Foxes, red, blue, and silver, passed. Weasels, ermine, and beaver wound in and out of the long parade.

Miss Hickory felt dizzy and as if she were losing her mind. When she felt warm breathing on her neck there, up-boughs, she almost fell out of the tree. But it was only Squirrel, who fairly barked in her ear:

"What did I tell you, Miss Hickory? Now will you believe me? I am off now. You had better hurry or you will be late."

As Squirrel started down-boughs, she had another surprise. He was not alone. He was accompanied by an ancient, feeble squirrel whose fur was thin in spots, and whose tail had lost its plume. He chattered up an introduction.

"My mother! She is here just for the celebration. Hurry, if you want to get there in time!"

"There is no need of haste." Miss Hickory did, however, scramble down-boughs. "The barn will wait for me." But Squirrel did not hear her. She was really somewhat alarmed at being alone on so splendid a night, and she almost coasted down her tree from one icy branch to another. Having reached the ground, she took her place at the end of the procession. An odd little creature with human hands, face, and a long curling tail was just ahead of her. He walked upright. Monkey turned to look at Miss Hickory, then raised one little hand toward the sky where a great blazing star in the East now outshone the moon. Then he sped on.

"All contrary to the Almanac," Miss Hickory said to herself. "No stars are bright in the full of the moon."

But she too, small and alone, trailed on in the light of the Christmas star until she reached the barn.

At once she found that she had waited too long. The barn door was open and inside, the home animals, Cow, Twin-Heifers, Old Horse, the fowls, the sheep and lambs, crowded. Mr. T. Willard-Brown wearing a smartly tied bow of red ribbon sat primly beside a circle of gray-gowned mice, not even sniffing at them. Owls perched blinking on the henroosts. Foxes mingled with the hens. Monkey hung by his tail from a beam. At the door of the barn a long-eared donkey stood patiently waiting, his eyes closed and his head drooping as if he had reached the end of a long journey. The camels also waited in the barnyard.

Miss Hickory darted around to the cathole, but however she tugged at it she could not open it. At last she crept in

and out of the maze of legs in the barnyard until she was just inside the barn door. She could go no farther. No one harmed her, but no one made a way. They all seemed to share a secret that she had been too stiff-minded to believe. So she waited there, and at midnight the Christmas star entered the barn. It shone straight down through the roof and made a line of gold that rested above Wild-Heifer's stall. There was suddenly a sound of rushing wings outside. Then the creatures, every one, kneeled down on the barn floor and bowed their heads: Cow, Old Horse, Twin-Heifers. Mr. T. Willard-Brown among the mice also bowed his head. Monkey folded his little hands. The camels' great heads drooped. Squirrel and his mother were near Miss Hickory.

"What is it?" she asked him. "I can't see." Squirrel pushed her head hard, but her neck was too stiff for bowing. "I told you," he whispered. "Wild-Heifer's manger holds—" But the sound of his voice was drowned by such a pealing of the icicles that Miss Hickory lost the last of his words. The creatures arose. They had all, except Miss Hickory, seen the golden imprint in Wild-Heifer's manger.

The light of the Christmas star faded and the procession of strange creatures formed and started back toward Temple Mountain. The barn door closed and there was again only her same snowy world, but it was Christmas morning. Miss Hickory started home. She met Fawn, who was feeding alone through the snow of the Acre-Piece. In High-Mowing the hen-pheasants of the Ladies' Aid Society were settling themselves beneath their bed quilt. Not a cock-pheasant was in sight. When she reached Squirrel's hole she peeped in. He also was alone, busily cracking the nuts that he should have been saving. Winter had still far to go.

"If I hadn't seen it, if I hadn't been there, I should say that I dreamed it," she thought. Then, all at once, Miss Hickory felt that something was really wrong with her. "I should have paid heed to Squirrel," she thought. "I might have seen inside the manger in the barn, but I was hardheaded." She felt sad and confused.

10. GROUND HOG SEES HIS SHADOW

GROUND HOG who lived in a hole at one end of the field called High-Mowing was a surly man. He had a mean disposition and no friends. Wearing an unbrushed ragged suit, he took his lonely way among cornstalks and bean poles, his small sharp eyes wary and his long yellow teeth ready for gnawing vegetables. All summer he ate sweet corn, tender peas, snap beans, new squash, and greens. He bit into fruit and then left it spoiled on the ground. He never gave a thought to his family, which included many children and grandchildren, but left them to forage for themselves. In fact, if Ground Hog ever met one of his relatives he bared his ugly teeth and tried to get to the vegetables first. And whatever he ate turned into fat, which made it possible for him to live without meals all winter.

So when the corn was made into sheaves, when the vegetable gardens were gone to stubble and the frosts came, Ground Hog retreated to the far end of his deep hole and went to sleep. Curled up in an untidy ball, he snored and dreamed of bigger and better crops another year.

His bad habits made Ground Hog unpopular. He had no friends and he was afraid; afraid of Quill Pig who frequented the same fields and gardens with his back full of barbed arrows all ready to shoot; afraid of guns; yes, and afraid of his shadow. Ground Hog was without any education whatever and his own shadow seemed to him like an enemy, dark and sinister. If Ground Hog ever saw his shadow he tried to flee from it. Of course the shadow went everywhere with him, but when he was stealing he seldom saw it, being concerned only with his stomach.

But now in February, when there was an occasional day of sunshine and the warmth penetrated within Ground Hog's earth bed, he would stir, yawn, feel of his empty stomach, then crawl over to his doorway and peer out.

Now, in February, this came to pass. There was an unexpected thaw. The sun rose earlier and set later above Temple Mountain and shone strong upon the orchard. Ground Hog felt the sun, felt his shrunken stomach and on a day in early February he poked his nose out of his hole. He could scarcely believe his eyes. Drip, drip, came the melting drops from the icy boughs of the apple trees. He dipped a paw into the snow and came to mud underneath. He ventured out a little way, then farther. Suddenly, however, he was frozen in his tracks with horror. Like a giant with open mouth and long teeth right beside him on the snow, Ground Hog saw his shadow. It looked larger and fiercer than it had last year.

Not only did he see his shadow, but close beside it stood a strange creature with a sharp nose, twig hands and feet, a rakish hat on the side of its head and a shrill voice.

"Halt!" said Miss Hickory.

Although she stood her ground, Miss Hickory too was scared. She had never seen Ground Hog before; he was as large as Mr. T. Willard-Brown and his teeth were formidable and close.

Ground Hog turned and ran. Into the depths of his hole he scurried. Miss Hickory ran too, now that the danger was past. She did not stop until she fairly tumbled into the feathery, crooning midst of the huddled hen-pheasants, still living together in their Ladies' Aid Society in the shelter of the High-Mowing wall. The hens scattered, then rallied to her rescue as they covered her with their soft wings. But they were surprised. Never had they seen Miss Hickory run away from anything.

"There, there, my dear," Hen-Pheasant clucked. "Don't tremble so. You are among friends and perfectly safe, but whatever is the matter?"

When her breath came Miss Hickory told them.

"I have just seen a wild animal! As large as the barn cat but with sharp yellow teeth! Right here, near you. In High-Mowing I met it."

"What was the animal doing?" Hen-Pheasant asked. "Did it chase you?"

"Indeed, no. It was digging at the door of a hole with its shadow beside it."

"And then?" Hen-Pheasant looked anxious.

"It ran when it saw me, straight back into its hole."

"So you thought that Old Ground Hog ran from *you!*" Hen-Pheasant, now President of the Ladies' Aid Society and much less timid, spoke firmly. "Do you know what happened? Ground Hog went back into his hole because he saw his shadow."

"And what of that?" Miss Hickory could scarcely believe her ears.

"Six weeks more of winter!" Hen-Pheasant moaned. "If Ground Hog comes out of his hole and the sun shines so that he sees his shadow, he goes back in again. For six weeks longer it snows, freezes, and blows."

"Six weeks more of winter!" all the other hen-pheasants moaned.

"What makes him do that? I find my shadow, on a night when the moon is high, very pleasant company."

"Becauses Ground Hog is afraid. He steals vegetables and he fancies that his shadow will catch him. He is never out of his hole unless he is off thieving. He keeps in the shade, away from his shadow as much as he can."

Miss Hickory's head ached. The matter was beyond her understanding. . . . But of late her stiff twig body had felt softer, her legs more nimble, and her hands more supple. It was as if fresh sap were arising to quicken her chilly limbs. And as she felt her sap rising, her nut head worked faster.

"And very wise of Ground Hog," she took up the conversation. "All thieves are afraid. Why does he steal, I ask you? Because he is hungry! What would you do for three meals a day if the farmer did not leave dried corn for you here at your nest? Look at your pile of uneaten corn. And more will be left here tomorrow."

"Have you a plan?" Hen-Pheasant asked.

"It is you hens of the Ladies' Aid Society who should know what your duty is in a case like this," she told them. "Ladies *Aid*, not just looking after yourselves like a lot of pigs."

"You mean that we should give away our corn?"

"And why not? Show Ground Hog a little neighborliness and perhaps he will return the deed."

For a space there was silence among the hen-pheasants. They were thinking. It had not occurred to them to do more than take care of themselves, but the winter had gone well with them. Although they had been deserted by their cocks they had found sanctuary there in High-Mowing and had been given food regularly.

"Come again another day. Give us time to think," they told Miss Hickory. It was too momentous a decision to make at once.

But the next day the icy wind kept Miss Hickory at home. After the wind there were several days of thick fog. The sun did not shine for two weeks, but on a cloudy day Miss Hickory went over once more to the Ladies' Aid Society. As soon as they saw her they began clucking, arguing among themselves.

"Hush up!" she told them. "This is no time to think of yourselves. Winter has lasted long enough, and if anything we can do will break it, let us do it." And with that she filled both hands with yellow kernels of dried corn from the hen-pheasants' pile. "Come on!" she ordered.

So each timid hen took a kernel of corn in her bill. One at a time, their President leading, they walked in a line behind Miss Hickory, away from their shelter, across High-Mowing, until they came to the place where Ground Hog slept. They knew that it was his hole, for they could hear his deep and regular snores.

"Spread the corn in front of his door," Miss Hickory told them. "Then run!"

They laid a square meal of corn in front of Ground Hog's hole. Miss Hickory rapped loudly on his door and they all scattered, but watched from a safe distance. Ground Hog's snores subsided. He stirred, unrolled himself, and they saw his homely face with shifty black eyes peer cautiously out. Then he came entirely out and pounced upon the corn, eating it greedily. He looked hither and yon, and since it was a dark day he saw no shadow. He closed his door and walked warily away from his hole, gnawing at the greening bushes that were pushing through the snow.

"Spring is coming!" Miss Hickory exclaimed.

"Spring is coming!" the hen-pheasants chorused, looking toward the woods where Cock-Pheasant and the other husbands had spent the winter.

As for Ground Hog, he did not return to his hole. He watched to see when the spring ploughing would begin. He made no effort to return the food he had been given. One could not tell whether he knew that he was a weather prophet. But the fact remained that he was.

11. MISS HICKORY TAKES TO THE AIR

A LOUD rushing of wings. A dark shadow across the sun like an eclipse. Loud-mouthed talk in the tops of the pine trees. So the crows returned. Now, in March, it was Old Crow Week. The young ones of the season before had grown as tough and noisy as their parents. The old ones, those in rusty black with worn tails and cracked voices, cawed harsh bass-notes in the chorus. There was still frost in the ground, snow lay in patches and the brooks were roofed with a thin layer of the winter's ice, but there was a change in the scene, a promise of spring in the air. Miss Hickory felt it in her twigs as from the look-out of her nest she watched the doings of Old Crow Week.

Not that she approved. Oh, no! And because one of the big shaggy birds looked exactly like every other one, she could not discover Crow among his fellows.

"He isn't here yet," she said to herself.

Then, as the flock with hoarse caws of delight plunged down among the frightened hens of the Ladies' Aid Society, gobbling their corn and sending the timid fowls scuttling away to safety, Miss Hickory thought:

"Crow is not here, I know. He isn't a bully and a thief."

But it was fascinating, she found, to watch the celebration from her lofty point of view. After they had stolen a large dinner, next on their program came the crows' battles for nests. All winter their great nests built of loosely placed branches in the tops of the pine trees had withstood the weather. Any self-respecting bird would want to build himself a new nest when he came back, but not the crows. With flapping wings and stabbing bills they fought for the old ones. Only those who could not steal a nest started off for building material. And as soon as a crow left a nest the fight began all over again.

Then, as the nests were finally patrolled by crow police, a committee headed by the toughest, noisiest crow of all began staking out claims. They boldly walked along behind plows and with their great yellow feet made marks at the edges of the fields where corn would be planted, little ground maps discernible from a tree only to a crow's sharp eyes. They left young crow scouts near truck gardens to watch for the first planting and to report when young beans, peas and asparagus could be nipped. And always the head man of the scouting committee urged them on to map more fields and gardens, cawing raucous important commands, never doing any work himself, and returning at sunset to the best and stoutest of last season's nests in the top of a great pine above the orchard.

"Undoubtedly a gangster," Miss Hickory decided after she had watched him every day of Old Crow Week. "He ought to be shot, but they'll never catch him. He's too wary." She stayed at home all that week, living on the hoard of her frozen foods. When Sunday came, at the end of Old Crow Week, she decided to make a trip to the woods to see if anything was green there. In a short time Jack-in-the-Pulpit might stretch his slender hands up through the mold. She had not heard a sermon all winter. So Miss Hickory took off her hat, brushed, straightened and pulled it on again, and was about to step out of her nest and start down-boughs when she was completely bowled over. Her nest almost turned upside down with the weight of two great yellow claws perched on its edge. Two wide rusty-black wings spread tent-wise above her. A rough, coarse voice cawed:

"Still here, old Nut? How is your sap running after the long winter?"

It was, without doubt, Crow. And as Miss Hickory clung to the sides of the nest, trembling, she saw to her horror that Crow, *her* Crow who had so kindly found her a home last autumn, was the leader of the Old Crow Week celebration. He it was who had led the raid on the Ladies' Aid Society, stolen corn, directed the mapping of the cornfields and now, without doubt, was going to commit murder. But as quickly as he had come, Crow hopped to a near-by branch of the apple tree. His voice softened.

"Dear lady, pardon the high spirits of an old resident. I just stopped by to see how you had passed the winter North. The Southland may be all right for birds who take cold easily. I go in that direction to pick cherries and certain kinds of garden stuff that do not ripen here until spring." He rolled his eyes and winked at her.

Now that he had removed his heavy weight and her nest had righted itself Miss Hickory stood up, indignation in every line of her twigs. New words popped into her head. "Scram! Vamoose!" she exclaimed shrilly. "I am sorry that I ever met you; thief, dastard, disturber of the peace!"

"*Dear* lady! So crotchety when spring is in the air! In like a lion, out like a lamb, as they say of March. But between you and me, it's in like a crow, out like a bluebird. You don't seem glad to have me back again, and I have just left an important committee meeting to invite you to take a flight with me."

Flight! The word changed Miss Hickory's rage to excitement in an instant. All her life she had regretted her inexperience in travel. Going away on a bus or a train, she had heard, broadened one's mind. As for taking an airplane, no one in all the years the Old Place had stood had done that.

"When? Where's the airport? Who'll buy me a ticket?"

"Now. Right here at your nest. Nothing to pay!" Crow answered all of her questions in one long caw. He came close, lifted Miss Hickory deftly in one claw, turned his head and dropped her on his broad back. "Hold close to my neck," he told her. She did that, clutching with both arms. Crow spread his wings, they arose in a rush of high air and were off. Crow made harsh but true statements as they flew.

"The same old Nut, judging by your remarks, making no allowances! Suppose I do eat the neighbors' corn? I eat bugs too. What if I can't sing like a thrush? I am the first bird to spread word of the spring thaws. And I have no hard feelings that I, Starling, English Sparrow, Hawk and Owl can be shot at whenever we can be found close enough."

"All right. All *right*, Crow!" She gasped as the bare trees raced along beside them and the brisk wind tossed her words like sparks from a bonfire. "Don't try to explain yourself. Just keep on going."

So Crow flew in a great wingspread, high, low, round about, here and there, carrying Miss Hickory so steadily that she had not a moment of airsickness.

Snow a foot deep still whitened the top of Temple Mountain, but at the foot a rose-pink haze lay in lovely color. That was the budding of the red maple trees. In the lee of the mountain there hung a golden curtain, as pale yellow as a new moon. That was the flowering of the willows. The earth was a checkerboard of farms marked off by their gray stone walls and patterned by brown furrows. Once, as Crow swooped down over High-Mowing, she saw some moving spots like bits of scattered broken sunset.

"Cock-Pheasant and the other men have come to collect

their wives," Crow explained. "They want help in making new-nests in the brush pile over in the woods; and you'll see, every one of the girls will forgive and forget now that mating time has come."

Sure enough, Crow was right. As each brilliant cock-pheasant left the entrance to the Ladies' Aid Society, at a spaced distance behind him walked a small drab hen, silent as was befitting, but her heart bursting with happiness.

Then up, up, flew Crow, until behind the tossing balloons of the March clouds Miss Hickory could see blue sky. Down, down, to listen to the faint but bright singing of faraway Third Brook, rippling beneath its broken ice. Barn-Heifer was out at pasture. Wild-Heifer, dragging the rope and post that had tied her in the barnyard, was charging through the woods beside Fawn, both of them big and longer of leg now. Up again and meeting newcomers; a yellow butterfly trying the wings that had been so lately folded in the blanket of the cocoon, a flock of early song sparrows, some lovelorn chickadees. She felt safe up there among the sunbeams. Miss Hickory was able to fly at last without holding Crow's neck. She stretched her arms wide in delight. Such motion! Such earth movies! Such promise of things to come! The moss that trimmed her winter garments, now brown and scraggly, blew off, but she let it go without a regret. Her hat also came off and blew away, a pinpoint of green below, then completely gone.

"Crow!" she shouted as they circled finally above her apple tree, "I shall make myself some new clothes."

"Atta girl!" he agreed coarsely.

"I shall clean house," she said, remembering her busy days of redding up her little corncob house when the lilacs budded.

"I wouldn't bother," he advised her. "Look at me, hale

and hearty, and I have never tidied my nest or even washed myself all my life!"

"Well," she thought, "do look at yourself; mud on your feet, dust on your wings, living in a last year's nest instead of a well-built new one." But all this mattered very little, she knew, weighed against Crow's kindness and courage.

"I'll be right over yonder," he told her as they dived and made a safe landing close to her nest in the apple tree. "If you need me, just whistle. Spring is early this year."

Miss Hickory, with breathless thanks, alighted. Crow spread his wings. Then a word used frequently in sermons by Jack-in-the-Pulpit came into her head.

"Glory be!" shouted Miss Hickory.

12. BULL FROG LOSES HIS CLOTHES

WHEN BULL FROG set out from his pond for Third Brook late in the autumn, he had a fixed idea in his slow-moving mind. Frog Pond had been his home for years. There, among many others of his family, he spent his summers sounding loud *ker-chunks,* in a booming voice, his springs bringing up hundreds of his tadpole children, and his winters sleeping in the warm mud of the bottom. If anyone had told him that this step he was taking, this long hop, was the beginning of a great adventure, Bull Frog would have rolled his goggle eyes in surprise. He was tired of being a target for stones, thrown at him by two-leggers when he came out to sit in the sun on the bank. They even broke the ice to try and torment him. After many years of having stones thrown at him, Bull Frog had decided to look for a new home.

Frog Pond, green with rushes and noisy with its croaking inhabitants, lay close to the Old Place. The bottom, thick with mud and a jungle of waterweeds, was a Paradise for frogs. *Croak. Ker-chunk. Boom. Boom.* They made as much noise as a swing band, and Bull Frog, a fat bespectacled old fellow, was the loudest bass of all. He was tougher and louder each season, a frog to be reckoned with as he sat on a little rostrum made of tin cans that had been thrown into the Frog Pond, and pleasantly shaded by water plants. His eyes bulged out like marbles and his suit of rough green skin with big humpy spots was so thick that it is questionable whether a stone would even have scratched it. But Bull Frog for time without end had heard the saying, "People who live in glass houses shouldn't throw stones." Surely a glass house would be safer. He had tried to set that proverb to croaks, hoped to be able to boom it out from the pond, but it had been beyond his powers. So after many years, in early autumn, Bull Frog had started out regardless of wind and weather, of the future, or of anything except that, a hop at a time, he was leaving Frog Pond behind in his search for a safer home, for a place where there were glass houses.

He found it slow going. One hop! Stop! Look all around with his dim popping eyes that were more used to seeing through water than through the forest. Another hop! And the farther he hopped the greater distance in the rear was his old home, the more difficult was the search to locate a new one. Bull Frog knew glass when he saw it, for once an old milk bottle had been thrown at him, splintering in pieces of transparent rainbow on the sunny rocks of the bank. But the longer he hopped the more impossible did it become to find anything in the woods that had the slightest appearance of glass. He found warm muddy holes beneath logs. He rested for the night in a homey swamp. He hopped due West following First Brook, then Second Brook, because of their good damp bogs, and no one disturbed him, for it was growing frosty and no one of importance to a frog was out. But days and weeks passed. The bugs on which he lived were scarce. His suit grew stiff, more nubbly, and lost its fresh green color. But at last, when the first frosts at night had begun, Bull Frog gave a great leap and found himself on the edge of Third Brook.

"Here," he gurgled to himself as he plunged deep into Third Brook and peered up at its glassy roof of clear water and paper-thin ice, "is a place where I shall not be disturbed." And it really seemed as if he were right. All along the bank lay the deep and silent forest. Darting dragonflies and little shining fish surrounded him. Over the stones the water bubbled and sparkled. It sang treble to Bull Frog's bass. He felt free of all responsibility; no more swarms of tadpoles to train, no more dodging stones. So Bull Frog stayed alone there in Third Brook. Almost every day he came out and sat on the bank, his long green legs and yellow shoes dabbling pleasantly in the cold water. His *boom, boom, boom* sounded faintly like a tom-tom in a little jungle of juniper, alder and tall ferns. But days passed and so did the weeks, each one frostier than the one before.

Now on April Fools' Day, the first day of April, it was still frosty. Although the sap was running, the swamps and streams were still icy. Most of the snow had melted, so Miss Hickory decided to have one last day of skating. What ice was left would be glary; it would hold up so small a person as she. So, early in the morning of April Fools' Day, she started out for Third Brook, a favorite skating stream of hers. She loved to skim up it, wondering where it began and who had taught it to sing.

The stillness there was pleasant, for the noise of Old Crow Week had been deafening. She reached Third Brook easily and was just about to glide off on the ice when she was startled by a faint but familiar *ker-chunk. Chunk. Chunk.* Miss Hickory had heard frogs about the Old Place. This sounded like one, but also like a frog in trouble. She followed the sound along the bank of Third Brook and came at last upon a sad and weathered figure.

Bull Frog's good green suit was cracked wide open in places and the material had faded to a dirty brown. His big head lay weakly on his chest and his eyes were covered by their thick eyelids. His mouth hung open, but every now and then he made a great effort, took a deep breath and said, "*Boom. Ker-chunk.*" Going closer, Miss Hickory saw what had happened. Bull Frog's legs were frozen tightly into the ice of Third Brook. Even now, with April thaws in the air, he could not break himself out. He was too weak.

"How did you get in such a state?" She pulled his big head upright but it flopped down again.

Bull Frog Loses His Clothes

"Glass house! *Ker-chunk*. Two-leggers stoned me. *Chunk*."

"I don't get you. Come to the point," she said briskly.

Bull Frog made a loud gurgling, gasped, and spoke with effort. There, frozen in Third Brook and covered with snow all winter, he had been thinking hard.

"Came over here from the Pond. People in glass houses don't throw stones. Got stuck here in the ice."

Again Bull Frog collapsed like an empty balloon.

"Stuff and nonsense!" Miss Hickory exclaimed. "The house makes no difference. It all depends upon how a two-legger was brought up whether he stones frogs or not. No one in my family ever did."

But it seemed as if her words were wasted. Not only did Bull Frog's head droop, but his whole body sagged. Miss Hickory came closer. It was alarming to see such dejection. She grasped Bull Frog firmly by his belt, braced her feet in the ooze of the bank, and pulled.

Bull Frog straightened himself somewhat. *Boom. Boom.* He held up his head and turned it toward her. "Pull harder!" he gasped.

"Well, help yourself then!" She felt something slipping in her arms. Bull Frog was a slippery fellow to hold, but she gripped him more tightly, pulled harder. "Wiggle your legs and the ice will crack."

Miss Hickory tugged and Bull Frog, his courage renewed, gave short leaps toward higher ground. Suddenly the ice cracked. Bull Frog got his legs out, leaped like an acrobat out of the water and up over Miss Hickory's head. She, poor

lady, sat down hard on a rock, not in relief but from shock. In her arms she held Bull Frog's clothes, all of them. His greenish stockings, his cracked and dingy trousers, belt and waistcoat. In pulling Bull Frog out, she had taken off all his wearing apparel; truly a calamity! She turned away, modestly dropped the clothes and was about to go home when a booming *Chunk! Chunk! Ker-Chunk!* made her look at Bull Frog.

He was transformed. He wore a fresh new suit, greener, yellower, more thickly spotted than the old one. And the old clothes were just vanishing in Bull Frog's mouth. His belt alone, like a length of spaghetti, dangled from one lip. He gave a mighty swallow and downed it. When he could croak, he explained:

"Always do this in the spring, but much obliged for your help. Take my old suit off, find a new one underneath, swallow what I can of the old one. So long, lady!" And with mighty hops he was off in the direction of Frog Pond, which seemed to him in memory a safer home than Third Brook had been.

Miss Hickory was so confused that she had trouble finding her way out of the woods. "They speak of eating one's hat," she thought, "but he ate a suit, from his skin out!" It was too bad that she had never heard of April Fools' Day. But her mind cleared at last in the fresh April shower that came up as she reached Acre-Piece and crossed into the orchard. In the distance Bull Frog's *Boom! Boom!* drummed in the spring. And Miss Hickory, remembering former springs, decided to clean her house next week.

13. HOMELESS AGAIN

ROBIN was a conceited, pompous fellow. One reason for this was his family nickname, Robin Redbreast; quite undeserved because his waistcoat was not red but a rusty orange. Another reason for Robin's vanity was the attention he always received when arrived North in early April.

"The first robin!" and "The early bird catches the worm!" were among the sayings that greeted him if he got home first, which he always tried to do. So Robin strutted over the grass of the Old Place, cocking his ear toward the ground to catch the sound of wriggling, dipping in, bringing up a worm and downing it whole, although he much preferred cherries. He was really showing off because he loved the notice he attracted. He knew that his name would be printed in the newspaper among the other arrivals from the South. He did not need his annual trip South, as he had excellent health and strong lungs. One of his cousins frequently stayed North in the deep pine woods all winter, but not Robin. Running the risk of being made into a pie, off he flew South every autumn and back in the spring just to satisfy his stomach and his pride. And now, with spring well started, he had returned, shivering, but determined to keep up his early-bird reputation.

He knew that the tree in which he had nested the year before was also remembered sentimentally. So he made a practice of going back to it before his mate insisted that he stop behaving like a clown and begin building. On this day in particular, now in April, a flock of early bluebirds had claimed more compliments than Robin and he flew over to the orchard, along McIntosh Lane, until he found the gnarled old apple tree with its bent and sheltering boughs where his nest had rested so safely last summer. There it was, still resting tight and strong in a crotch of the boughs. But as Robin alighted on the rim of his old nest he had a great surprise.

When Miss Hickory cleaned house she did it thoroughly. The first April showers had softened the mud with which her nest had been plastered, so she patted and smoothed it. She had laid long strips of smooth bark across protruding twigs of the nest for shelves, and she brushed off these shelves and rearranged what berries and rose hips were left from her winter's store of frozen foods. She threw away her old bedding of leaves and down, and replaced it with the soft curling buds of the new ferns that were coming up along the banks of the three brooks. As a last touch, she shaped a little bowl of clay, and when a shower had filled it she put a bunch of very early Mayflowers in it to make her nest bloom with the spring. As she was in the midst of this house cleaning Crow flew over and stopped by.

"Good work!" Crow cawed, peering down inside. "I have warned all my pals against trespassing here. Is there anything I can do for you?"

"Not a thing, thank you, unless you can advise me about my spring wardrobe." Miss Hickory looked coquettish, then scowled in disapproval at Crow's untidy suit. He dropped his head in shame. "I plan to take a bath next month," he said. He turned to fly, but Miss Hickory called:

"When does school open, Crow? I may apply for the job of teacher. I taught Hen-Pheasant how to quilt."

"Open!" Crow jeered. "It will close in two moons now. School has been keeping all winter when I was away. The time for playing has come, longer days and sunny weather."

"Then I must make myself a play-suit," she said, but to herself, for Crow was off again.

Miss Hickory was very much in need of new clothes. Her head was dangerously bare since she had lost her hat. Her dress was in shreds, and there were holes in her coat. She set off immediately for stuffs, and although the old pine needles were brittle and the new ones bent as she sewed and

knitted, she did contrive to outfit herself very well. There were enough new leaves to stitch into a short skirt, and new green grass for knitting herself a sweater. Although very little hat material was to be found, she shaped a large bonnet of wild cherry blossoms. Her hands, limber and quick, flew. As a finishing touch, she slipped her hard little feet into a pair of pink lady's slippers.

"They will wear out quickly," she thought, "but I will carry them when I take a long walk. Jack-in-the-Pulpit will be holding Sunday services soon. His green hands are just showing through the ground in the swamp. He will admire me in pink slippers."

So the days went by, and Miss Hickory did not go home to McIntosh Lane for a week. Checkerberry leaves, tender and spicy, made her meals, and an old acorn cup held clear brook water when she was thirsty. Her legs that showed to the knees below her short play-skirt seemed more shapely, brown, and plumper than last spring.

"I believe I am growing!" she thought. "Anyway, I am much more limber."

Indeed Miss Hickory looked sprightly and smart as she started home, her lady's slippers hung by a length of grass around her neck to save them. All the way there were signs of an early spring, red maples in full bloom, willows turning yellow, young lambs frisking in Acre-Piece, a greening light on Temple Mountain. As she came to her tree and swung by a low branch to the one next higher, as she started climbing up-boughs, she felt extraordinarily happy. She thought how much nicer a nest was than her corncob house that had broken up in a severe ice storm last winter. Even if it had lasted another season, she decided, she would not have returned to it. Climbing, thinking, feeling contented, she did not see until she was right beside it that her nest was occupied. A bunchy ball of feathers with a sharply beaked head sat inside. Robin, whose wife it was sitting there on eggs, perched as a guard on a branch close by, looking ridiculous with a long worm hanging out of his mouth.

In the instant that Miss Hickory's shock made her dumb, Robin dropped his worm. He swelled out his waistcoat, opened his bill fiercely and flew at her. She swung to another limb, broke off a twig and shook it at him.

"Get out! What do you mean by taking my nest? Go away, both of you!"

"*Your* nest! Who gathered the twigs and brought the mud

a mouthful at a time? Who made it strong enough to last all winter? Who stole it and lived in it?"

Arguments, Miss Hickory knew, that she could not answer. "I cleaned it for the spring," she said in a low voice.

"*And* paid no rent!" Robin scolded. "Do you know the proper name for a person like you who settles into an empty nest that he did not build? *Cow-Bird!*"

That sounded shameful to Miss Hickory, if true. But she was grief-stricken. All seemed lost: her view of Temple Mountain, the stars at night, the forest by day, her apple-tree housekeeping, most of all, her safety. She tried again.

"I thought that birds always built new nests in the spring."

"So they do, but when I find an old nest in as good shape as this one, I move in. We have a head start now in eggs. The children will be hatched and down before those of any other bird for miles around. News, that! We shall get another newspaper notice."

Still Miss Hickory lingered. "Then, if I stay around, if I wait, I could perhaps have the nest later?" she ventured.

Robin went into a rage. He flew at her, pecking. "No! Go away! I may raise a second family. Don't dare to come up this tree again!"

Miss Hickory went down-boughs in haste, losing her bonnet on the way. This was the first time in her whole life that she had felt really hopeless. Crow was too rugged a man to come to her rescue a second time. He would feel, she knew, that she should, after such a good winter, be able to settle her own affairs. Chipmunk would live untidily all summer in the ruins of the corncob house. Mr. T. Willard-Brown was too busy in the barn to help her and, also, he was a selfish person. Far above her in the apple tree Miss Hickory could hear Robin in a burst of song, fairly gloating over her.

"Cheer-up! Cheer-i-o! The early bird! Cheer-up!" he sang.

Miss Hickory reached the earth and looked about on all sides. Everything was springlike. Violets bloomed in purple delight. The dandelions were golden pennies spread as far as she could see. Yet here she was, her new bonnet lost, and her beautiful pair of pink lady's slippers far above her where she had lost them, too, in her hurry of coming down-boughs.

Suddenly she had a plan. For the last moon she had not heard Squirrel scampering about, cracking nuts, down here in his hole at the roots of her tree. Very likely, she decided, Squirrel had moved. His hole would be a pleasant home for her, cool in summer and cozy next winter. Miss Hickory peered into the darkness of the hole, listened, then stepped in.

14. SQUIRREL TAKES REVENGE

Miss Hickory was unable to see her hand before her face at first because it was so dark inside Squirrel's hole. It appeared, though, as she became used to the dimness, a large and gloomy place. The floor was covered with cracked nut shells, and as she stepped carefully among them she did not come upon a single whole nut. She might not have noticed what appeared to be an empty and ragged gray fur coat lying in a far corner, but the rattling of the shells as she made her way roused Squirrel. He lifted himself.

"Who's that?" Squirrel asked in a faint voice.

She went close and poked him with her foot. "Just what was in my mind to ask," she said. "Why, it's you, Squirrel. You appear to be in a state of ill health."

"Starving! That's what I am; starving to death." Squirrel leaned limply against the wall of his hole. "Not a nut left." Was it her imagination or did he fix his eyes on her head? She backed away and spoke sternly to him.

"What became of that large store of nuts that was here last fall?"

"I ate them," he replied simply.

"*And* the woods full of nuts that you could have buried?" she went on bitterly.

"I told you about those at the time," he spoke patiently. "My memory is poor. Often, the very moment I buried a nut, the very second that I turned my back on it, I forgot where it was. I did well to bring what nuts I did home. When the first thaw came I started out, ill as I was, to try and find a few that I had buried. Could I locate them? No, not one!" He sank down to the floor again.

"I told you last fall and I tell you again, Squirrel," Miss Hickory shook a finger at him, "that you are a witless fellow. Why didn't you use your head? A brainless wastrel, that's what you are!"

"Wastrel?" Squirrel jumped up, his rage giving him strength. "Do you know that if it were not for the nuts I bury and then forget, there would not be so many new nut trees in the woods? I plant trees, whether I mean to or not!

"Use my head, did you ask? What, I beg of you to explain, is the matter with your head, Old Nut, that you feel you can blame me, call me witless? Well—" Miss Hickory could not move in fright as Squirrel lunged forward and put a heavy paw on her shoulder—"they say that two heads are better than one. All this time I have spared you. Oh, I knew all about hickory nuts, so juicy and full of sweet meat, but I waited as long as possible. Now I must act. I hope you will understand," he finished jokingly, "that this hurts me more than it does you."

And with that final bitter remark Squirrel took off Miss Hickory's head and put it in his mouth.

Strange as it seems, although separated from her body and beginning to crack in Squirrel's sharp teeth, Miss Hickory's head went right on thinking. In fact it seemed to think faster than it ever had before, and aloud.

Crack! "I never was a very useful head. Or perhaps it was the poor use to which you put me. A nut was not the proper headpiece for so tough a body as yours."

Crack. Crack! "Too hardheaded you were altogether!" As Squirrel crunched the head it talked fast to Miss Hickory. "In the first place you wouldn't realize how important a change of scene is until you were deserted, until Crow had practically to move you, against your will, to Robin's nest for the winter.

"Fancy, too, all the good adventures your hard head made you miss. You wouldn't believe Mr. T. Willard-Brown when he invited you to see Cow being given a dose of medicine.

You wouldn't believe Squirrel, here, when he told you about
the Christmas Eve celebration in the barn. That was the
worst of all your mistakes. You were too late in reaching the
barn. You did not see the wonder in the manger there on
Christmas Eve."

Crack. Crack. Crack! Now, almost eaten by Squirrel, there
was little left of Miss Hickory's head to talk to her. It made

one final effort and spoke. "Think what a pleasant life you've had. Sunsets and a mountain to look at! Good clothes from the forest and so many friends! Plenty to eat for the picking! The neighbors kind to you! And what have you ever done for anybody else? Oh, I grant that you did found a Ladies' Aid Society, but that pleased your vanity. You lived selfishly all your life. You wouldn't even give away your hard head." But the voice of the nut broke off. It was completely cracked and eaten.

Feeling her way, Miss Hickory groped and stumbled out of Squirrel's hole. She had lost her head, but not her arms and legs. For some strange reason, her body felt more alert and capable than when it had been hampered by a nut head. As her feet crossed the threshold of Squirrel's hole, that gentleman's every hair stood on end in horror. Seeing Miss Hickory's headless body moving, erect and brisk, gave him such a shock that he chattered to himself for days and when he decided at last that he had only dreamed the ghost-walking of his friend, he reformed. He repented of having eaten Miss Hickory's head and was a good squirrel forever after, gathering enough nuts for each winter and eating only three meals a day, with nothing between meals.

On she went, her twig feet feeling familiar stones and grass, her twig hands touching the bark of the old apple tree that she knew as home. If Miss Hickory's head had been on it would have discouraged her. It might have spoken thus:

"Robin will peck you! You can't see your lady's slippers

anyway, if that is what you are looking for. Lie down on the
grass here and dry up." Those are the words the nut head
would have spoken. But, without a brain, Miss Hickory gave
vent to her feelings. There was not a drop of doubt or fear
now in her freely running sap. She set one foot in a toehold
of the rough bark of the apple tree, caught the tip of a low
bough with both hands and grasped it firmly. She gave a
high kick and a swing, higher than she had ever dared to
swing before. Now she caught the next higher bough, gripped it, and swung again. Up-boughs went headless, heed-
less, happy Miss Hickory.

The entire climb was pleasant. She knew from long living
there all the apple tree's crooks and crotches. She felt the
warm wind from the South. She threw away her spring
clothes, sorry to do it, but she could climb better without
them. Robin was so astonished when she reached the nest
that he flew into the deep woods. His wife left to get worms
and that delayed the egg-hatching for a week. In the mean-
time another robin received a newspaper notice about his
early babies. But when Miss Hickory reached her old nest,
she only touched the blue eggs gently and then moved on.
The situation of the nest was too shady, too sheltered. She
felt the need of a higher location in the apple tree where the
sun would be stronger, the winds higher and the rains could
be her shower bath.

She was surprised that she could climb so far, but the old
apple tree grew every which way, gnarled and at angles.
Every bough and twig felt like home to Miss Hickory, who

had lived among them so long. It never entered her mind, since she now had none, that she might be going too far, climbing too high. As she climbed and swung, higher and higher, she could feel the sun on her body like a cloak of fiery gold; and the spring breezes coming down the mountain, across the lee, over the orchard, blew her up, up, as if she had wings.

Miss Hickory had another feeling, strange and unexplainable. She felt knobby, as if she were budding. Her warm sap, like lifeblood, seemed bursting through her body and as she went on, higher and higher toward the top of the tree, she had a feeling of being really at home, as if she belonged there. All the way her hands found similar bumpy places on the tree's boughs. Finally when she had left her nest, Squirrel, High-Mowing, all of her past life below, far down on the earth, she began to feel somewhat tired. Even sleepy! Her twig feet and hands found a wide upper crotch in the apple tree. She pushed herself into it and, calling it a day, Miss Hickory rested there.

15. ANYTHING CAN HAPPEN

Now, in May, the Old Place had opened its doors. The grandfather clock with the big brass pendulum ticked again, tick-tock, tick-tock, time without end. The white towel that had wrapped the Bible was folded and put away. The Old Farmer's Almanac, opened at the May, Fifth-Month, page, hung or the wall. Through the windows came a lovely perfume, for the lilacs were in bloom.

Ann, who had come home early from school in Boston, looked underneath the lilac bush at the ruins of a little house that Timothy-of-the-Next-Farm had made for her of corn-cobs. She looked at it sadly, for the doll whose body was an apple-tree branch and whose head was a hickory nut with a sharply pointed nose, was gone.

Timothy came along, along, whistling. "What's the matter, Ann? Lost something?" He too looked beneath the lilac bush.

"Miss Hickory!" Ann told him. "She is gone. And her home that you made for me is broken up."

"Well, we've had a hard winter," he told her. "Snow five feet deep, ice storms. You couldn't expect that little house to stand up."

"But Miss Hickory?" Ann was close to tears. "She's completely gone. You'd think, Timothy, that parts of her would be left in these ruins."

"Now, you listen to me, Ann!" Timothy said, "You're too old to play with dolls. I'm too busy with the spring chores to make you another playhouse. Just forget the whole thing."

Ann turned on Timothy. "I can't forget Miss Hickory. She wasn't just a doll. She was a real person, born and bred in New Hampshire. I don't forget my friends, Timothy, and you ought to know that."

There was no accounting for girls, he thought. He put his hands in his overall pockets and whistled. Far away, but answering him, there came a hoarse *caw, caw* from the direction of the orchard.

"Crow!" Timothy explained. "He'll be talking to us before the summer's over."

"Birds don't talk." Ann said.

"Crow does, or at least he makes himself understood," Timothy told her. "He's been places and seen life. He's a leader. And when he hears me whistle, if he has anything important to tell me, he answers back."

"Such as?" Ann sounded skeptical.

"Well," Timothy said reasonably, "if you don't believe me, if you think Crow's just talking through his hat, come along and see. Let's take a walk up through the orchard, Ann."

A walk through an orchard. Through an orchard when the apple trees are in bloom! The Sleeping Beauty has awakened there. Daphne, dressed in her new draperies, flutters a welcome to Persephone returning with her hands full of violets. The Bluebird darts down with pieces of Heaven on his wings. Anything wonderful can happen in an orchard.

Ann and Timothy, side by side, crossed the road, and there on the far stone wall of the field called High-Mowing sat an old crow in dingy black, uttering hoarse words as loudly as he could. When he saw the boy and girl he flew, cawing, farther on.

"He does sound as if he had something to say," Ann agreed as they followed him.

"*And* likes to hear himself say it!" Timothy chuckled, then whistled. *Caw! Caw!* Crow's answer came back to them from the sidehill of the orchard where the McIntosh apples grew.

"Everything points to a good McIntosh year," Timothy went on. "Last year it was the Baldwins that yielded and the McIntoshes rested. Just look at their bloom!"

They stood awhile, looking at the beauty of the apple

blossoms. Pink and white, all around and above Ann and Timothy, the orchard, as far as they could see, was blooming. It hung a pink curtain against the new green of Temple Mountain. All the worn crotches and ragged elbows of the gnarled trees were covered with blossoms, but Timothy was right. The McIntosh trees had the thickest, the loveliest bloom of all.

They followed the rows of trees, Timothy talking like a farmer, showing off to Ann.

"I always say there's nothing like our New Hampshire McIntoshes; there's an apple for you! Big, bright red, juicy, sweet-smelling! Crunchy when you bite into it. Pretty in the middle of a table. Quick-roasting in front of the fireplace on a cold evening."

"Timothy, stop!" Ann laughed. "You make me too hungry."

"Well," he told her, "I don't want you to think that there's nothing here in the country to come back to."

"Why, Timothy, there's everything!" Ann took his hand— "except Miss Hickory."

But he interrupted her. "Here's a tree I've always liked, an old McIntosh that hasn't been pruned or grafted in I don't know how long. They thought it wasn't worth it. My grandfather planted it. But look at the old thing now! If it isn't blooming thicker than I ever saw it before!"

They stopped in front of an elderly McIntosh tree, so low and widely branched that one could easily swing into it from the ground and climb up-boughs. Timothy whistled. Crow answered harshly from above.

"Where is Crow?" Ann asked.

"I don't know. I'll climb up and see," Timothy said, swinging carefully so as not to hurt the blossoms along the boughs of the McIntosh tree. He whistled. Crow cawed loudly. Timothy followed Crow's call until he came to a high blooming branch that pointed off yonder toward the mountain. It was pinker than pink. It fluttered and danced like a ballerina. Crow sat just above.

"Whee!" Timothy shouted down to Ann, "I've found something up here. Can you climb up?"

"Climb up!" Crow spoke quite plainly. "Easy does it! *Caw! Caw!*"

Taking care not to hurt the blossoms, Ann swung, then carefully stepped from one bough to another, almost as if she were climbing a ladder. Crow balanced flapping and cawing above. When Ann came close to Timothy, he called excitedly, "Look here!" He pointed to the most flowery of all the branches. "It's a *scion!* It's growing like anything! But who put it in, I ask you? Not me, or anybody else so far as I've heard."

Ann looked. She saw the new dancing branch, its two arms, its slim little waist, its two legs, all garlanded with pink bloom. But it had a firm place in the apple tree there, held close in a crotch where the wind had broken the old bough and left a little sap-filled crack.

"A scion?" Ann asked.

"Sure! That's what a new graft is called, put into an old tree to start it blooming and bearing again. But we usually

tape it in until it begins to grow on the old branch, and that takes time. I don't understand. We didn't do any grafting this spring, and especially not on this backnumber of a McIntosh."

Perched on a bough, Ann gently touched the blossoming scion. She thought, but did not say, "It looks like Miss Hickory, up to the neck. But she had a head."

"Will it go on growing, have an apple maybe?" Ann asked aloud.

"Bound to!" Timothy said. "This scion is so much at home in this tree now that it will buck up the whole tree, give it a new start. But what I don't understand is—"

Timothy's words were taken out of his mouth by Crow, who flew off toward the pine woods, talking in harsh laughter as he went. *"Caw! Caw! Haw-haw!* Two-leggers! Think they can explain everything that goes on outdoors!"

Anything Can Happen

As for Miss Hickory, who had been a scion all along without knowing it, she felt completely happy. She would never have to do any hard thinking again. She had a permanent home at last and some day she would give Ann, who had recognized her, a big red apple.

CAROLYN SHERWIN BAILEY

Carolyn Sherwin Bailey was born in Hoosick Falls, New York, and spent her childhood in the little Hudson River town of Lansingburg, where she prepared for college at the local academy. She graduated from Teachers College, Columbia University, studied at the New York School of Social Work and in Rome, and then began writing—an activity which eventually produced thirty-five books.

The author and her husband, Dr. Eben C. Hill, lived for many years on Hill Farm, in Temple, New Hampshire, whose antiques and apple orchard inspired Miss Bailey's Newbery Award-winning book about the apple-twig doll, *Miss Hickory*.

NEWBERY AWARD BOOKS
AND NEWBERY HONOR BOOKS
AVAILABLE IN PUFFIN

Adam of the Road *by Elizabeth Janet Gray*
Amos Fortune *by Elizabeth Janet Yates*
The Avion My Uncle Flew *by Cyrus Fisher*
Blue Willow *by Doris Gates*
The Corn Grows Ripe *by Dorothy Rhoads*
Daughter of the Mountains *by Louise Rankin*
Dobry *by Monica Shannon*
Dogsong *by Gary Paulsen*
The Ear, the Eye, and the Arm, *by Nancy Farmer*
Figgs & Phantoms *by Ellen Raskin*
Fog Magic *by Julia L. Sauer*
The Golden Goblet *by Eloise Jarvis McGraw*
The Good Master *written and illustrated by Kate Seredy*
The Hundred Penny Box *by Sharon Bell Mathis*
The Journey Outside *by Mary Q. Steele*
The Light at Tern Rock *by Julia Sauer*
Miss Hickory *by Carolyn Sherwin Bailey*
Moccasin Trail *by Eloise Jarvis McGraw*
My Side of the Mountain *by Jean Craighead George*
The Perilous Gard *by Elizabeth Marie Pope*
Rabbit Hill *written and illustrated by Robert Lawson*
Rascal *by Sterling North*
Red Sails to Capri *by Ann Weil*
The Road From Home *by David Kherdian*
Roller Skates *by Ruth Sawyer*
Roll of Thunder, Hear My Cry *by Mildred D. Taylor*
Tree of Freedom *by Rebecca Caudill*
The Twenty-One Balloons *by William Pène du Bois*
The Secret of the Andes *by Ann Nolan Clark*
The Silver Pencil *by Alice Dalgliesh*
The Singing Tree *by Kate Seredy*
A String in the Harp *by Nancy Bond*
The Summer of the Swans *by Betsy Byars*
Upon the Head of the Goat *by Aranka Siegal*
The Westing Game *by Ellen Raskin*
The White Stag *written and illustrated by Kate Seredy*